THE VIRTUAL BOSS

A Novel
by
Floyd Kemske

CATBIRD PRESS

CATBIRD PRESS, 16 Windsor Road, North Haven, CT 06473
Our books are distributed to the trade by
Independent Publishers Group.

First Edition

Library of Congress Cataloging-in-Publication Data

Kemske, Floyd, 1947-
The virtual boss / by Floyd Kemske.
p. cm.
ISBN 0-945774-22-2 : $19.95
1. Computer software industry--United States--Fiction.
2. Computers--Fiction. I. Title.
PS3561.E4226V57 1993
813'.54--dc20   93-8479 CIP

For Jan and Barbara,
who, from page one,
knew there was a novel
in there somewhere

And for Mom,
who, from day one,
knew there was a writer
in there somewhere.

ONE

ARTHUR wanted his boss to like him. He didn't want a grand display of affection. He just wanted to be liked. He wanted a small gesture or a low-key remark that would show some respect for him as a human being. But his boss did not seem to have much patience with concepts like respect. In fact, his boss was virtual and didn't have much patience with anything human. This was made plain to Arthur the morning all the trouble started.

He was staring at his screen, trying to remember what he had meant by the file name "CORRECT.DC1." A magenta box appeared in the center of the screen. His keyboard locked up, so he just watched as the box expanded until it overlaid his work. Then words formed in green characters, which created an unexpected rock-candy effect on the magenta.

—*Where's that report you promised me, Art?*

A putrid feeling in the pit of his stomach told Arthur he had missed a deadline.

—*I was just finishing it up,* he typed, stalling.

He touched return, and both the message and his reply vanished, to be replaced an instant later by a new question.

—*When are you going to send it to me?*

—*In half an hour,* he typed. He cleared the window again with his return key.

*—You'd better not be blowing smoke up my ass, Art. I
hate it when you blow smoke up my ass.*
—I'll have it for you in half an hour, he typed.
—OK.

And the window winked out, leaving Arthur staring
again at his file directory.

He sighed, then caught himself. He stood up and looked
over the wall of the cubicle to see if anybody was around
to hear him. Linda was hunched toward her screen, apparently unaware of him or anything else in the world besides
her work. Her blouse had come out over her waistband in
back, and Arthur noticed that strands of her short hair
stuck out over her right ear, as if she'd slept on it wrong.
She was scraping her mouse rapidly around the surface of
the desk, heedless of it bumping into the piles of papers
and notes around her. The display changed rapidly, and
Arthur could see she was opening and closing volumes,
directories, subdirectories, files. She seemed to spend most
of her time looking for things among those files of hers.

He looked in the other two cubicles of the hub, and they
were empty. Richard and Aaron were each off coordinating
somewhere. He sat down and sighed again, being careful
this time to keep it quiet. It was not the kind of company
where you let other people hear you sigh. It was the kind
of company where you kept your feelings (and almost anything else, for that matter) to yourself. It was the kind of
place that suited Arthur well.

He didn't want to send the report to his boss. It wasn't
ready yet. It needed confirmation in two critical areas. But
the files he needed were in use, so he couldn't access them
through the system. And he certainly couldn't call anyone
on the telephone, it being a serious breach of company
etiquette to call a meat person directly for information. He
would just have to take a chance with the estimates he had
used in preparing his rough draft.

Arthur felt bad about the deadline. He wished his boss

were a little more understanding about such things. His boss knew how to invade any partition of his machine, including Arthur's personal workspace. He did so a dozen times a day, both here at the office and on the terminal he kept in a little den off his living room at home. Arthur sometimes thought his private life was limited to the hours from 23:00 to 03:00, when his boss slept. He had always thought it a little strange that software actually had to sleep, but he was grateful for it. He knew if his boss didn't sleep, he wouldn't either.

For the other twenty hours of the day, Arthur could hear from his boss at any time. And during business hours, he heard from him constantly, as the intrusive window— sometimes magenta, sometimes lime green, sometimes bright yellow—appeared on his screen and froze whatever he was working on. Arthur would then stop whatever he was doing (physically and mentally) and make himself available for a "meeting."

The two of them probably could have gotten by on far fewer meetings if his boss were better organized. But his boss was apparently incapable of storing up his thoughts and questions for unified presentation. No sooner had he got an idea or run across some bit of information than he had to talk with Arthur about it. His boss, even while having access on the company's massively parallel hardware system to the most precise chronometric programs in existence, had no sense of time and no skills in the area of time management.

Arthur called up the report file and looked it over. It wasn't very long. His boss didn't like long reports. He started to give the command to send it to Library Eight of his boss's "office." Then he checked himself when he realized he still had at least fifteen minutes left before the report was expected.

He leaned back in his chair, clasped his hands behind

his head, and stared at the acoustical tiles that formed the office ceiling.

Arthur was part of what was known as the Production Project—a complex of relationships among people and software packages both inside and outside the company. In the old days, when Arthur first arrived at the company, it had had departments. But a couple years after the arrival of the new CEO, Donald F. Jones, the company was reorganized into projects. When that happened, most of the company's department heads, including Arthur's old boss, left. A lot of meat people left the company in those days.

It was an uncertain time for Arthur, who knew neither whom he was supposed to report to nor what he was responsible for. But the uncertainty didn't last long. He began receiving messages on his terminal that suggested work assignments and let him know how he was doing.

As Arthur answered whatever questions appeared on his machine and did as he was told, the messages began to acquire a style. He found it convenient to think of the messages as coming from a sort of virtual person. As he interacted with it over weeks and months, the personality behind the messages became more distinct. Eventually, it developed enough of an identity to become a character in the stage play of Arthur's life. In those early days, his boss was friendly and avuncular and would actually ask to confer with him:

—*Got a minute, Art?*

This boss was the first person ever to address him as "Art." They often had long conversations in those days— about management, product quality, customer relations. Arthur felt he had a relationship with someone at the highest level of company management. And his boss seemed to assume the role of advisor and mentor in all areas of Arthur's life, which was, admittedly, pretty much centered on his job. Arthur found it easy to be completely open with the person he perceived to be inside his machine.

He even sought the boss's advice on major purchases and leisure activities. The boss, of course, had little to say about such human preoccupations, but Arthur often found that talking it out with him helped him to formulate his thinking.

Even Arthur's mistakes strengthened the bond between them. The Consolidated Corporation matter had been the first assignment for which he'd taken major responsibility. And he'd done very well with it, meeting all the deadlines, keeping everyone informed via the e-mail system, and documenting the costs in minute detail. When he reviewed his costs, however, he realized he had screwed up.

He had used a broker to get a module he could have bought directly from one of his contract vendors. The result was a fifteen-hundred-dollar premium on a piece of information that was not even critical to the final product. All because he didn't check the existing contracts. He knew he'd never make that mistake again.

He had gone to his boss to confess and apologize for his fifteen-hundred-dollar error, but his boss would have none of it.

—*Don't apologize, Art. You're worth $1500 more now.*

Characteristically, his boss had summarized several pages of reasoning in a single sentence. Arthur could not help but feel he was enjoying a positive relationship with a software system.

That all seemed a long time ago now.

Out of the corner of his eye, Arthur saw movement on the screen, and he knew his boss was back. He rocked himself back to the keyboard and struck his knee on the desk. His boss's message this time was in black characters against magenta. At least it was easier to read.

—*Well?*

—*I was just finishing up*, Arthur typed.

He reached down and rubbed his knee. He would have a bruise there later.

—You haven't made a keystroke in three minutes. What are you doing?

—I spilled some coffee, typed Arthur. *I'm sending the file now.*

The window winked out again.

Arthur invoked the "send" command and watched the graphic—a white circle that filled itself with narrow red slices—report the progress of the transmission. It went quickly.

As soon as the pie filled, it disappeared and the magenta window reappeared. His boss must have had some sort of aesthetic inspiration, because this time the message started at the center and grew outwards in both directions at once.

—What is this shit, Art? Where are the savings on direct costs?

Arthur blinked at the message for a moment, then started to type before his boss might have a chance to elaborate.

—As you can see, he typed, *I am proposing we make all our reductions on indirect.*

—Of course I can see that, asshole. It's the goddam direct that's killing me.

—The shorter cycle will use less staff time and increase productivity, Arthur typed back.

—I need a 10% reduction on direct.

—I don't see how we can accomplish that without changing our vendor contracts, Arthur typed.

—And?

—Are you saying I should drop a vendor? Arthur typed.

—I'm saying you should reduce direct, Art. Figure it out for yourself.

—I don't have any vendor contracts coming up for renewal, typed Arthur. *The only way I can drop one is to break it.*

—Are you a candy ass or what, Art?

"You're being unreasonable," Arthur whispered to the screen. His boss couldn't hear him, of course, but it made him feel a little better to say it.

—*Are you ordering me to break a contract?* he typed.

—*I'm not ordering you to do anything. All I'm doing is concluding this meeting by telling you your goddam report doesn't do what it was supposed to do and you're not performing up to spec.*

—*I can't do that to a vendor*, Arthur typed.

But then he realized he was typing into his own workspace. His boss's window was gone.

"Shit!" said Arthur. He banged his fist on the desk beside the keyboard. Then he felt embarrassed. He hated it when he swore.

He stood up to see if Linda had heard him. She was looking straight at him. She had her back to the terminal now, but she was still slouched in her chair. She was toying with her mouse, flipping it in the air by its cord. She caught the mouse in her hand when she saw him and smiled buoyantly with bright, white teeth, the two frontmost ones separated by a gap just wide enough to accommodate the corner of a diskette. She pointed the mouse at him.

"Squeak," she said.

Arthur smiled back as if he weren't embarrassed, and sat down. He felt the knot of his necktie to see if it was straight, although he couldn't really tell by feel. He wished he had a little mirror in his cubicle. Linda could do with some orthodontia; it was unusual for a woman to have so little self-consciousness about something like that.

"Frustrating, isn't it, Arthur?" she said over the partition.

"Yeah." Arthur tried to make the word sound like it had a laugh in it.

"Me, too," she said. "Sometimes it's like talking to an echo."

"Yeah." Arthur wondered what she meant by that.

Although Linda didn't seem to fit into the corporate culture, Arthur couldn't help but be attracted to her. Of course, the attraction never got beyond the level of fantasy. Arthur wanted love more than anything else in the world, but he couldn't risk being rejected by Linda, and even if he ultimately had some success in establishing a relationship, he knew it would put his job at risk. It was that kind of company.

Arthur had ten vendor contracts, each of which represented a meat person known to him personally. His boss was ordering him to terminate one of these contracts. It was an idea just this side of unthinkable.

Arthur pulled open his desk drawer and took out a pad of lined paper.

The top sheet was a handwritten resignation memo, in Arthur's precise printing, addressed to Donald F. Jones, the company's chief executive officer. He reread it, then set the pad down on his desk, picked up his pen, and crossed out the words "very real." He wrote "unmitigated" right above them. He reread the memo and thought about the effect it would have on Donald F. Jones. None at all, probably. The company had over three hundred employees. What was one project coordinator, more or less? He sighed and put the pad back in his desk drawer. He would never send the memo. Revising it occasionally gave him a harmless little fantasy, a tiny bit of emotional relief in the struggle to remain gainfully employed.

He looked at the time display on the menu bar and saw that he could reasonably clock out for a few minutes and call it breakfast. His boss didn't understand breakfast, but he tolerated it. Arthur wasn't hungry. He just felt he needed to get away from his machine and relax for a few minutes. He checked for messages that might have come in while his workstation was under the buffer. Thankfully, there were none. He invoked the script for clocking out, which would send a message to the company's monitoring system to show he was away for twenty minutes. The exact number of these absences he could take in a day was a matter of judgment, as was nearly everything regarding his work hours and habits. But his rule of thumb was four in the course of his twelve-hour day.

While the machine was retrieving the clock-out script, he stood up and took his suit coat from the corner of the cubicle partition, where it had been hanging by the collar. He slid his arms into its sleeves and tried to seat it comfortably on his shoulders, which was impossible. He had bought a designer suit in a moment of weakness, and now it reminded him, every time he put it on, that he did not have a designer body. He reached over to touch the function key that would start the script he had called up.

The clock-out script would renew his buffer so that it would continue to record messages. It wouldn't disable his beeper, of course, but his boss usually didn't search for him when he was on break, so he thought he might have some time to himself to calm down.

The clock-out script began accessing files and issuing commands, typing out the standard message for signaling a break, opening a communications window, and sending the message. Then it opened his calendar to record the time, flashing briefly past the pages for the current week, red entries showing appointments and black ones activities to date. He couldn't actually read the display, of course, because it went by so fast, but he thought he noticed the deadline for the report he'd just filed.

It was tomorrow's date.

* * *

Twelve hours after his deadline fiasco, Arthur was standing in a long line at the one operational banking machine in the subway station. The two other machines were down: one of them was covered with a slatted metal pull-down

that said "SORRY. TEMPORARILY OUT OF SERVICE."
The other had had its small screen punched out, whether
by a vandal or a disgruntled depositor, Arthur didn't know.

Arthur was clutching his salary check and a deposit
envelope and trying not to watch the man in the dark blue
suit who was slowly pushing buttons on the one healthy
machine. Arthur was no more comfortable watching someone use a banking machine than he would have been
watching him use the next urinal.

"You got a dollar?"

There was a man with an unpleasant smell standing
next to him. Arthur didn't look at the man, but he glanced
at his outstretched hand, which looked as if it hadn't been
washed for a year. He shook his head and kept his eyes on
the floor.

"Bless you," the man said and shuffled away.

They really ought to do something about the unemployed. But there were so many of them, how could they?
Arthur thought about how lucky he was to have a job.

He could see from the corner of his eye that the man at
the banking machine was reading each instruction and
carefully selecting the buttons to push on the keypad. Most
banking machine users learned from experience not to
trust themselves to work the machine hurriedly, since the
menu screens were rarely the same from use to use. They
changed at least daily to accommodate advertisements and
service messages, so you had to pay attention in order not
to transfer money to the wrong place or make unintended
purchases.

The man had a white handkerchief wrapped over his
finger, and he dabbed at the buttons as if he were cleaning
them. There was something wrong with the speaker, so the
machine honked instead of beeping as he touched the
buttons. The front of the machine was caked with grime,
and even the buttons on the keypad had some sort of crud

around their edges. Arthur felt in his pocket for his hand-kerchief. His knee throbbed a little.

He didn't like standing in line very much, but his bank's billing cycle ended at 20:00, and if he didn't deposit his salary before then he would get extra charges on his chronic overdraft. He wondered if other people in the company spent as much on overdraft charges as he did. He had no idea. He had no notion of other people's salaries. It was not the kind of company where people talked about their salaries. He had worked next to Linda for over two years, and he didn't know if she was married or lived alone, had a boyfriend or was gay, and each possibility supported a completely different set of fantasies about her.

About the only thing he knew about Linda was that she had an infectious laugh. She laughed just about any time he spoke to her. He had to admit that he'd become quite fond of her laugh, so much so that he found himself trying to make jokes for her. Today, they had encountered one another in the elevator. They had both gotten on at the fourth floor to go down, and the elevator took them up to the fifth. Linda said she thought something was wrong with the elevator, and they both got off and waited on the fifth floor for another car. Arthur made a remark about having an elevating experience, and she not only laughed, but she continued to giggle after the elevator arrived and they got in. Arthur smiled at the memory, then looked around to see if anyone had seen.

There were three people in line in front of him and five behind. Much of the employed world was in the same rather urgent financial position he was in. His company had a direct deposit system, but Arthur preferred to handle his check and put it into his account himself. He simply didn't trust electronic funds transfer. He had enough trouble with software that he didn't need to invite more.

An outbound train roared into the station and emptied itself. The man at the machine anxiously finished his transaction, glancing back and forth at the train while the machine's printer wrote his receipt, and grabbed his card as soon as it emerged from the slot. He stuffed his handkerchief in his pocket, gathered up his briefcase from the floor beside him, and sprinted toward the train. His printed receipt fell to the platform with the rest of the subway trash.

Looking rather pleased with himself, the man hopped into the car before it sounded its warning bell. The doors slid closed and the train roared away, sucking a pile of receipts toward Arthur's feet. A woman took the man's place at the banking machine, and the line of people moved forward a step, like convicts on a chain gang. Arthur watched the red lights on the back of the train as it disappeared into the tunnel, and listened to the woman tapping the keys of the banking machine. Honk honk honk.

He looked surreptitiously at the other people waiting. All of them seemed slightly bowed and grimly stolid. But what else could he expect at ten minutes to twenty hundred in the evening? The only people who would do their banking here on the subway platform were commuters, and the only people who commuted at twenty hundred were dedicated employees. Arthur knew from experience that there is very little joy in life for dedicated employees.

The woman at the machine finished her transaction, took her card, and left. The next person took her place.

Arthur thought about having a talk with his boss about the deadline misunderstanding. After all, his boss should be made to understand that he has to respect the deadlines he himself has set up.

He wondered how his boss would react to such a confrontation. How could he defend himself? What could he possibly say when Arthur told him that the calendar showed the deadline for the report to be a day later than he had demanded it? Arthur knew exactly what he would say.

He would say the calendar was wrong.

The next person left, the drift of printed receipts on the floor got a little deeper, and Arthur shuffled absently forward.

Another train roared into the station. Its doors made grinding noises as they opened. A crowd of people got off, and a crowd of people got on. The warning bell pealed, the doors ground shut, and the train thundered away. Trash swirled along the platform.

Arthur looked up. It was his turn at the machine. He walked up to the tiny screen and was pleased to see by the continuous time display that it was still three minutes to twenty hundred. He was going to beat the overdraft charges for the first time in six months. He inserted his card into the slot, wrapped his handkerchief over his forefinger, and began entering his PIN. Honk honk honk. The welcome screen cleared and the next menu appeared. An amber message was centered in the small dark screen, surrounded by a rotating marquee of flashing uppercase X's.

—GOT A MINUTE, ART?

"What is this?" said Arthur.

Then he realized there were people behind him and he must look silly talking to himself. Arthur didn't know how to deal with the message. He started to shake his head, then thought better of it. The border around the message continued to flash as the machine waited patiently for his response. Obviously some kind of interactive advertisement.

The screen didn't give him any choice to make. He pressed the "CANCEL" key. Honk.

The screen cleared and the message was replaced by a new one, which also had a flashing marquee around it.

—I WANT YOU TO DO SOMETHING ABOUT THE
  DIRECT COSTS ON YOUR PROJECT. GOT THAT?

Arthur stood staring at the machine. He had a weak

feeling in his bowels. He didn't know how long he stood there without doing anything, but he heard the people in line behind him begin to shuffle anxiously. Finally, somebody spoke.

"Are you going to be there all night?"

"Sorry," Arthur said without turning around. He jabbed at the "CANCEL" key. Honk.

The screen cleared, and a new message appeared inside the flashing border of X's.

—*COME ON NOW, ART. USE YOUR IMAGINATION, MAN. YOU'LL HAVE TO SPELL OUT YOUR RESPONSES ON THE KEYPAD.*

Arthur looked over the keypad. It was like a telephone keypad: each button had a large number in the center and three small letters on top.

There was more shuffling and a little coughing behind him. A train rumbled into the station, and its doors squealed open. The center of the screen cleared, and a new message appeared.

—*USE THE ALPHA CHARACTERS, ART. I CAN FIGURE IT OUT.*

Arthur began to laboriously spell out a reply, wondering how his boss would ever be able to make sense of it. The train roared out of the station, and Arthur could sense frustration building in the line behind him.

—*GHI ABC MNO MNO MNO MNO WXY WXY ABC WXY GHI MNO MNO DEF*, he typed, longhand for "I am on my way home."

The screen cleared and filled with a new message.

—*I CAN SEE THAT, ART. TELL ME SOMETHING I DON'T KNOW. DO YOU UNDERSTAND WHAT I MEAN ABOUT DIRECT COSTS?*

Arthur sighed again.

—*WXY DEF PRS*, he typed.

The screen cleared and another message appeared.

Somebody in the line behind him spoke. "What are you doing up there? Some people here want to get home."

"I'm sorry," Arthur said to the little screen. "The machine's acting funny."

"Oh, great," said the voice. "That's all I need. First the Gibson account, then the old man's tantrum. Now this. What else are you going to do to me, God?"

Somebody tittered. Arthur wanted to get away from there. The screen cleared, and a new message appeared.

—*GOOD. DIRECT COSTS, ART. THAT'S WHAT I NEED. CALL ME AS SOON AS YOU GET HOME AND WE CAN TALK ABOUT IT.*

"Three trains I've missed now," said the voice. "All because my goddam bank can't keep its goddam banking machines in good repair. Are you almost done up there, mister?"

"Just finishing up." Arthur touched in his reply.

—*MNO JKL*, he typed.

The screen cleared again, and another message appeared.

—*ALL RIGHT, THEN. I'LL TALK TO YOU LATER. YOU SHOULD DO SOMETHING ABOUT YOUR OVERDRAFT. YOU JUST GOT HIT WITH ANOTHER CHARGE. MAYBE YOU SHOULD TRY DIRECT DEPOSIT.*

Then the message winked out and was replaced by the familiar banking menu with its choices for withdrawal, deposit, and account transfers. The continuous time display said 20:01. Arthur punched the "CANCEL" key and took his card. He stepped away from the machine, and the next person eagerly took his place, punching the keypad rapidly. Honk honk honk.

Arthur slipped his card and his undeposited salary check into his jacket pocket and walked over to the waiting area of the platform. He stood back toward the wall, away from the crowd. A train rumbled into the station, its doors screeched open, and people sluiced purposefully onto the platform.

He decided to let this one go and take the next one.

Two

THE elevator slowed, then stopped. "This is five," it said.

Jones suppressed the urge to say, "Thank you."

His office was on the sixth floor, but he always got off at five, walked across the building, and climbed the stairs. It was partly for the exercise and partly to stay in touch with the rest of the company. He was the only one who worked on the sixth floor.

The elevator door opened, and two employees were standing there waiting. One was Linda. Jones was surprised. She worked on the fourth floor. This was one of the reasons he always got off on the fifth. The other employee was someone Jones didn't recognize, a man in an ill-fitting suit. The man had just said something, and Linda was laughing. She stopped when she saw Jones.

"Hello," said Jones. He hoped he didn't sound or look awkward. He stepped out of the elevator and smiled at her. Then he smiled at the man who was with her.

Linda didn't say anything. She went into the elevator with the man, and Jones had the distinct impression that she started giggling as the doors closed. That wasn't like her. He had never thought of Linda as a giggler. She had a lively sense of humor, but she never giggled. In all the years he'd known her, even quite intimately at one point, she'd never giggled. What did giggling mean? He made a mental note to check on her work and performance.

Jones looked up the corridor and saw a pair of employees, dressed as if for the beach, watching him. He smiled.

"Good morning," he beamed.

"Good morning, Donald," they said in unison, then split up to return to their workstations.

He squared his shoulders under his English suit, the one with sleeve buttons that actually fastened and unfastened, and set off for his office at the other end of the building. He hummed a tune and swung his briefcase just a little.

The floor was a wide corral of workstations. Individually decorated by their occupants, they varied in appearance from the spartan to the sybaritic. About half the cubicles were occupied, it being only 10:00 a.m. The inhabitants studied computer screens or tapped at keyboards. They dressed in varied and sometimes chaotic ways that made the place look a little more like a carnival or a rock concert than an office. Everyone who saw him spoke when he walked past.

"Good morning, Donald."

"Hey, Donald."

"Hello, Donald."

He smiled broadly at each and made supportive gestures, pointing a thumb or a fist into the air as if they were all members of a winning team, which, after all, they were. He knew none of their names and recognized no more than a quarter of them. They all seemed to want a piece of him, but isn't that what corporate management is all about? As far as he was concerned, they could have as many pieces as they wanted if they kept the numbers up. He imagined himself waltzing through the office, leaving a finger here, a toe there, an ear, a tooth, a testicle. He would give them anything they wanted in return for good numbers.

He got to the other side of the building, pulled open the

fire door to the stairwell, and bounced up the steps to the sixth floor. When he emerged, the floor was semi-dark, as usual. He walked down the corridor, quietly lined with mahogany paneling, and the carpet thickened under his step as he passed the conference rooms and offices of the executive suite. The offices were all empty; over the past two years, the company's executive staff had gone the way of the organization chart, the personnel policies, and the activity reports. Jones was the only one in the company who had an office. He was the company's only manager.

He walked through the empty outer office, where his secretary used to sit in the old days, and retrieved the incoming contracts left on the desk by the courier services. He tucked the colorful pasteboard envelopes under his arm while he entered the security sequence on the keypad next to the door. The green LED glowed, and he heard the bolt slip back. When he pushed the door open, the room lights winked on, and he entered, leaving the door ajar. He felt no need to close himself in. None of the other offices on this floor were occupied, giving him ample privacy even with the door wide open.

"Hello," he said to the machinery.

He heard the soft click of the coffee machine starting itself as he walked toward his expansive walnut desk. The hard drive in the workstation behind the desk whispered as the computer began booting itself for him.

He set his briefcase on the desk while trying to manage the courier envelopes, and they all spilled helter skelter. He sat down in his chair, looked at the mess on his desk, and momentarily allowed himself the luxury of trying to remember what it had been like when he had human servants. There still were people in his position who kept servants: egos in domestically-made suits who kept secretaries and administrative assistants to sit outside their offices and take care of things like pouring the coffee and arranging the courier packages neatly on their desks.

Jones's company, however, was averaging over $600,000 in annual sales per employee, not one of whom poured anyone else's coffee or arranged things on anyone else's desk. Pouring coffee and doing other people's housekeeping was not only undignified, it was unproductive. The executives who presided over such goings-on were doomed. They would perish before the competitive onslaught of Jones and managers like him.

He began to open the contracts, pulling apart the pasteboard envelopes and fishing out the papers, which he then piled in a neat stack for Harold, whenever he arrived with the scanner. Contrary to the predictions of the last generation's visionaries, automation had not cut down on paperwork. It had only increased it. One of the major preoccupations of business systems designers, in fact, was how to get the information on all the papers into the computer systems. At Jones's company, they had worked out an inelegant but reliable system: an employee whose job it was to take a scanner on a cart from desk to desk throughout the company, all day long. The solution had required a good deal less capitalization than installing scanners at every desk, and Jones had been able to invest in the most powerful dedicated scanner on the market. It could read and make sense of anything that was printed with a fair degree of precision, from handwritten notes to faxes. This resulted in a lot fewer complaints from the information system, which had to consolidate, file, and sometimes act on the material.

"Donald," said the coffee machine.

He turned in his chair and pulled out a cup of hot liquid. He sipped, then turned to his keyboard and his screen, which was now lit and waiting for him. He set his coffee cup down beside the keyboard and typed in his user name.

—*dfjones*

The security system reacted instantly. A beige window

with a delicate blue border appeared, and a question in large black letters typed itself into the window.

—*First item in your victory log?*

He shook his head and smiled. He would never get used to personal questioning by a computer. But it was a first-rate security system, and it would accept him as Donald F. Jones only if he knew things about Donald F. Jones that nobody else could know. He typed his answer.

—*Bronze medal, Bicycle Time Trial, Masters Heart Pacer.*

The medal, which was under his socks in his dresser drawer at home, wasn't much to look at. The bronze plating had worn down in places to some indeterminate metal, and the ribbon had fallen off—he couldn't remember when. But two years ago, when he broke it off with Linda and life seemed like it couldn't get any bleaker, he had sat down to compile his personal victory log, and it was the first thing he thought of. He took another sip of his coffee.

He pressed return, the window cleared, and a new question appeared.

—*Most difficult experience of adult life?*

—*Failure in sales,* he typed.

—*Personal life goal?*

—*To remake the modern workplace,* he typed. Sometimes he was astonished at his own hubris.

Satisfied he was Jones, the system engaged his personal workspace and presented a summary of the company's current goals:

—*Achieve $700,000 in sales per employee.*

—*Introduce all new products entirely from current cash flow.*

—*Provide ten-year expansion capability for management system.*

This last item had been suggested by the management system itself, which was obviously feeling cramped as it built its databases and enhanced its statistical reality models.

Jones read the items carefully, even though he'd read them daily for the past three months. They were good and rational goals, and he knew he would have reason to be pleased with himself when he met them. Life had taken on an ineffable bleakness since he had overcome the major obstacles to the company's success. But it was a bleakness he felt comfortable with, and he would not have given it up for anything.

He pressed return to summon his work window, and the system presented him with a menu of choices for reviewing, storing, calculating, or communicating. He chose "review," pressed return, and watched as four numbers, fresh as of 7:00 a.m., appeared.

—YTD SALES	*74.27*
—PREV YTD SALES	*60.57*
—EMPLOYEES (CURRENT)	*306*
—EMPLOYEES (PREV YR)	*297*

He pulled open his desk drawer and took out a pad of lined paper on which he had written a column of twelve dates and twelve numbers. He looked at last Monday's number and compared it to today's. The number of employees had increased by one. He put the pad back in his desk drawer and tapped the escape key to clear his screen. The top menu returned, but he pressed the page-down key to move his cursor to the blank area of the screen.

—*Why was an additional employee authorized?* he typed. The reply came as soon as he pressed the return key.

—*There will be an opening in an administrative project within the next 30 days. Workforce will return to previous level at that time.*

He pressed return and opened an e-mail file. The system prompted him, and he asked it to prepare a welcome message for the new employee. He typed in "dfjones" for a signature and tapped the return key. He knew that before the top menu came back, the system would have composed whatever message would make the new person feel most at home and would have placed it in the employee's work file.

When the top menu came back, he selected review again and continued his routine by checking all the company's major changes of the past day. What does any manager need to know, he often asked himself, besides the current number of employees, the current level of sales, and the most recent changes? He selected "Changes" from the menu presented to him. The system worked for a moment or two, then presented another screen.

—*The system has tracked 1513 changes in the past 24 hours. Of these, 3 have tripped internal delimiters:*
   1. *The Production Project has signed an additional contractor, bringing its total to 10.*
   2. *A member of the sales project has exceeded revenue budget by 25%.*
   3. *The Information Services Project coordinator has been sorted to Category 5.*

That last one was disturbing. The information services project coordinator was Linda. Category Five was the system's designation for plateaued personnel. Did this have anything to do with her giggling in the hallway? He realized he would have to look into this.

But first things first. Jones asked for the identity of the salesperson who was so far over budget, and the system returned the name "Wendell Santos." Jones was not surprised. It had long since ceased to be a source of wonder to Jones that the same names turn up again and again in any performance measures. Wendell Santos might wear a safety pin through his nose and talk like he was implanted with a thesaurus, but he could sell. He was probably one of the best hires Jones had ever made.

He turned from the terminal screen to his desk, reached

across the blotter, and pulled a sheet of notepaper from the holder. He uncapped his fountain pen and wrote the name on it. He stared at it for a moment, then wrote "25% over budget" beneath the name and tucked the piece of paper into the pocket at the corner of his blotter.

He stared at the piece of paper, peeking out from the leather pocket at the corner of his blotter. Anyone who could exceed his project's revenue budget by twenty-five percent deserved some kind of recognition for it, but Jones always hesitated at the idea of special recognition. It's not that it made him uncomfortable recognizing and complimenting people—there was no part of effective management that made him uncomfortable. But he worried about sending mixed messages to the employees.

The employees received regular feedback from the management software, and if he stepped into the process he could easily throw the delicate action-feedback-response system out of balance. He would end up with a group of employees working for him rather than working for themselves, which would disrupt everything he'd been trying to create at this company. The last thing he wanted was people working for other people, even him. The fundamental law of the workplace, Jones knew, was that when you put people in charge of other people, they would begin acting like . . . people.

But twenty-five percent over budget is a magnificent achievement, and Jones's hypothalamus told him to send a memo. He usually listened when the organ spoke to him like this. It had made quite a few of his successful decisions and, in a lifetime of sparing counsel, had won his trust. He told the system he wanted to write a memo, and it opened another e-mail window. He wanted to write his own message to Wendell Santos. He tapped out the first line on the keyboard.

—*The system just told me you exceeded your project's revenue budget by 25%.*

He sat back and read it. He shrugged. His hypothalamus told him to make it a recognition note. No directives, no policy, no encouragement, no hesitation, it said. Just recognition from the company's leader. He typed "FGJ" at the end. He sent it off, watching it disappear, those final initials fixed in his mind's eye even after the screen was gone.

It was rare for Jones to write a memo to an employee. It was rarer still for him to use the expression "FGJ." The employees thought FGJ meant "fuzzy good job," a reference to the slang expression "warm fuzzy." Let them think that. It certainly would have given a laugh to the man Jones learned the expression from. He smiled to think of one of the greatest teachers he had ever encountered. An utter barbarian, the man had taught Jones a great deal about management, primarily through the medium of the bad example.

He returned to his keyboard, went back to his workspace in the system, and typed in a command.

—*Commencing 04.14, set a system alarm and give me daily reports on sales by Wendell Santos.*

He saved the instruction under the name "activity monitor 04.13" and sent it to the system. An animated image of a cartoon soldier appeared in the upper portion of the screen, saluted, and disappeared. He needed some sort of acknowledgment from the system when he gave it an instruction, but he found this one irritating. It was amusing the first time he'd seen it, but it got old quickly, and he sometimes wondered whether Linda, who had installed it, intended it as a sort of personal affront. But he hadn't brought this company to its current sales level by taking note of personal affronts, intentional or otherwise. They could burn him in effigy if they kept their numbers up.

The system waited for his next command. He brought up the Changes screen again and reread the messages, studying the one about the Production Project's contractors.

When he was setting up the controls for this year's business activity, he had been concerned about the company's dependence on outsiders. It was true that using contractors gave the company speed and flexibility, and it reduced costs as well. But he was bothered that so many of the company's operations shared proprietary information with people who were really nothing more than strangers. As a first step in a long-range plan to reduce dependence on outsiders, he had instructed the system to monitor the number of contractors associated with every one of the company's projects and control those that seemed excessive. When the system asked him for a number to put into the monitoring program, he didn't know what to choose because he'd had no experience yet of what might be appropriate. He chose nine because it was the number of his favorite constitutional amendment. You have to start somewhere. Now the system was reporting that the Production Project had exceeded the limit. Jones wondered if he should look into it, maybe issue an override.

In the old days, if he found out one of the departments had exceeded his guideline on the number of contractors, he would have to go around and talk to the department head and try to find out what was going on. Then he would have to make a decision about whether an extra contractor was warranted in the situation. And if he decided it wasn't, he would have to let the department head know and instruct him or her to reduce the number of contractors. This would probably take three to four long conversations filled with wheedling and cajoling, and Jones would be made to feel his principles and philosophy were on the line. Then there was the matter of working it through an entire department, because the department head always seemed to need help with something like that. And that wasn't even the worst part. The worst part was the follow-up monitoring to make sure what ultimately happened was what he had decided should happen.

In the old days, management was just about the hardest work there was. But now, if he did nothing, the system would simply bring everything back into line and get the Production Project's contractors back down to nine. He wasn't exactly sure how it did those things, but it certainly saved a lot of wear and tear on him. He decided to forget about the override and let it go. Why second-guess his own decisions? It occurred to him that for matters like this, he wasn't even necessary at all, an idea so absurd it made him laugh out loud.

He didn't laugh too long, however. It was time to get serious and find out what was going on with Linda.

—*What happened to the IS project coordinator?*

—*Activity pattern identified as inconsistent with success.*

Jones stared at the message. Strange feelings raged inside him. He had known Linda for almost ten years. She was a top-flight technical person and an excellent employee. His affair with her had disrupted and nearly ruined his life. He had not realized he was capable of feeling, or inflicting, such pain. They hadn't talked much in the past two years. They mostly tried to stay out of each other's way. Fortunately, they had little need to interact. The supervisory software, after all, was self-maintaining.

Jones knew Linda was very busy running the projects to upgrade the system's hardware, but he assumed she was still operating at the same level of competence that he had always expected from her. Then again, he had also assumed she respected the culture of privacy he had tried to develop here, and after seeing her in a giggling conversation with another employee, he had to wonder.

If Linda had plateaued, it was a serious matter indeed. Jones thought about writing her a short note. But he had no idea what to say. All things considered, he knew the system could handle the problem better than he could. He shrugged and cleared the screen to bring up yesterday's stock closings and check on the system's buy-sell activity.

Three

HER body jolted itself against the mattress, and Linda came awake in the dark, groaning out loud, delivered from her nightmare. Sweat made her pajama top cling to her breasts; she was breathing hard, and her heart was racing. She pushed the blanket away, put her hand on her chest, and waited for her heart to slow. She was vaguely embarrassed, but as she collected herself she realized she was home, alone in her bedroom, and she could groan all she wanted. Then she remembered the nightmare and understood where the embarrassment came from.

There was a dinner party, at which she was the hostess, and she had moved heavily, as if she were under water. She couldn't remember the faces of the people around the table. She couldn't even say if they had any faces at all. They shifted identity without notice, so that she might be talking to someone she thought was her roommate from college, who would suddenly turn into her mother, her brother, or somebody she'd met briefly in high school. One of these conversations was interrupted by a neatly dressed man, who had approached Linda at the table and said, "Did you bring the Fruit Loops, Linda? They're all expecting Fruit Loops."

She had not been frightened by the neatly dressed man. As usual, he had been very civilized in speech and manner.

But she knew he was right: everybody expected Fruit Loops and she didn't have any. How could she possibly have been so thoughtless as to invite everybody over for Fruit Loops when she didn't have any? She was so ashamed she couldn't look the neatly dressed man in the face (not that he had one, of course). She just groaned and fell down. When her body struck the floor, she woke.

She lay quietly for a moment, trying to relax. She had been having a lot of bad dreams lately. Always the same. A neatly dressed man would appear to her in various bizarre settings and tell her, in one way or another, that she wasn't measuring up. She would be filled with a dread verging on panic.

The dreams were bad enough: the goofy situations, the shame, the panic. The worst part, however, was that the neatly dressed man was a pretty reliable premonition. His messages were meaningless, but the fact of his showing up always meant something was wrong at work.

The dark bedroom was suffused with a blue glow from the digital clock on the night table. Linda looked at it: 3:00 a.m. The last time this had happened, a month ago, the neatly dressed man had appeared to her in a surrealistic airport lobby to say she had missed her tryout and now she would never become a dancer.

Linda had never thought about becoming a dancer before, but she had awakened from that one with tears coursing down her face. The realization that she could *never* become a dancer was so final that it made her whole life seem a disappointment. She missed her plane.

The next day, she had still been trying to shake the feeling of shame that sat solidly on her chest when she discovered that she'd overlooked the lease buyout on the delivery contract, in spite of Chuck's explicit reminder to check it. She winced at the realization.

She wiped her forehead with her pajama sleeve, looked at the dark ceiling, and wondered what the neatly dressed man's message could mean this time. But she was too rattled to dredge up any of the details of her work from her silt-filled mind. She swung herself out of bed and grabbed her glasses from the night table. She took her robe from the bedpost and went downstairs to make herself some coffee.

The mechanical act of retrieving the coffee paraphernalia from the various cabinets in the tiny kitchen relaxed her mind somewhat. She took the package of coffee bags from one cabinet and got the beaker from another. The great thing about living for a long time in a place by yourself is that you know exactly where everything is. You can live much of your life on automatic pilot and keep your mind on important things. Like where you're going with your job. She turned around to the refrigerator and got out the milk.

While she was filling the beaker with water from the tap, it occurred to her that she should consolidate the coffee things. There must be a lot of wasted movement going from cabinet to cabinet to drawer to refrigerator, as the Bastard had so often and so ungraciously reminded her. He had always said she was disorderly enough to be dangerous, although he also said he loved her for it. What a laugh!

She remembered the day he called it off. He had stood in the doorway of this very condo, his patent-leather hair shining under the hall light, the dimple in his quietly floral necktie perfectly centered. As if saying a silent good-bye, he had looked around at the two-storey windows in the living room, the slate floor in the foyer, the circular stairway up to the loft bedroom.

"I made a mistake," he said.

He looked stricken when he said it. Linda made up her mind that she wouldn't let it be easy for him. She didn't speak, but waited for him to continue.

He sighed. "Don't worry. I owe it to you to protect you. It won't affect your job."

It was the exact wrong thing to say to Linda.

"Like hell it won't," she said. "I quit."

He didn't answer. He just looked pained, then turned and went out the door.

She winced at the memory. Yes, she'd been a fool to get involved with him that way, but what did he take her for, a *dependent* fool? Did he think she needed his protection? What a shithead! She didn't need anyone's protection.

She wished she'd been able to make good on her resignation, but there were so few jobs anywhere. She shrugged. It was two years ago. She had adjusted. Well, at least after the attacks had stopped.

The attacks started about a week after the Bastard had ended it. She was sitting on the sofa with the want ads, and she suddenly realized she had to make an effort to breathe. In a panic she called an ambulance, and they came and rushed her to the emergency room of the local hospital. They put a little clear plastic cup over her nose that fed her an oxygen-rich air mixture through some clear plastic tubes, and they began testing her. Several x-rays, blood tests, and some other procedures she didn't have a name for turned up nothing. The attack ended long before the tests did, and they finally recommended she see a therapist and sent her home.

She put off calling a therapist. Then she forgot all about it until the next attack. That was a difficult one. It came, once again, in the evening, at home, while she was reading the want ads. She felt she had used up her credibility with the emergency room, so she lay on the floor, barely able to breathe, and resigned herself to dying. Somehow, she survived it. The next day, she found a therapist in the Yellow Pages, called, and made an appointment. Three days later, when her appointment came around, she was feeling fine, so she called again and canceled it.

The next attack was shorter. They never got to be a matter of routine, but when she realized that they always happened to her when she read the want ads, she stopped reading them. After a while, they went away.

The beaker was filled with water. She turned off the spigot. Medical science indeed. They give you x-rays and blood tests, and then they tell you to see a therapist.

She stood in front of the zapper, entered fifteen seconds on its keypad, and thought about the Bastard. She saw him in his shirtsleeves with his necktie and suspenders, making the bed. He was a remarkable man: confident, certain of life and reality, fastidious, and voracious in his sexual appetites. She had known him for several years before they ever went to bed together, and in all that time he'd never given any hint of how enormous his sex drive was.

"Ready," said the zapper.

She absently took the little beaker out of the zapper and began to pour the hot water over the coffee bag in her mug. The steam rose from the cup and, with it, a stray thought that explained her nightmare and the appearance of the neatly dressed man.

She hadn't reviewed the test results of the read-write loops on the new optical processor. That was why the neatly dressed man had asked her for Fruit Loops.

It wasn't a serious error, just one of those things that makes you smack your forehead with the palm of your hand. The total cost would probably be a three-hour delay in a six-month project. Big deal. It could have happened to anybody. But she realized with a start that she was quite irritated with it all. She never made mistakes like this when she was still a developer. But when the system had become self-developing and she had been put in the position of a kind of project manager, these stupid little errors began creeping into her work. She often felt as if she didn't have enough to do, but she knew that wasn't true. If she didn't have enough to do, surely she'd be able to handle these matters without so many mistakes.

She wondered how Chuck would react to her mistake. She took a sip of coffee and burned her tongue.

It was difficult to think of Chuck as anything other than a person, even though Linda herself was the one who had written and debugged the major elements of his interface. But now that she was no longer in control of him, dealing with him was more like being supervised by a human being than working with software. She understood his various components—the processing elements of his learning engine, the rulebase that constructed his meaning representations and created his database queries, the screen painter that allowed him to make different effects on a screen—but he was endlessly changeable.

Linda had no sentimentality where Chuck was concerned, however. Her feelings toward him were the same as she would have toward any piece of software. Only he wasn't as easy to use; in fact, she felt less like a user with him than with any other software. His core coding— thousands of processing elements Linda thought of as the "learning engine"—made him adapt to each user, so she didn't feel she was using Chuck as much as being used by his ability to adapt himself to her.

When she first got him up and running, Linda had worked with Chuck for three months in a secure partition of the company's network, giving him cases and records and shaping his language and interactions into an entity she felt comfortable with. When he had enough background to become fully self-grading, she backed him up to tape, then reinstalled him on the primary volume of the corporate-wide system.

She remembered the empty feeling she had had after that. Once he'd been released, he assumed responsibility for his own maintenance, and he didn't need her anymore. It felt . . . well . . . funny. As she'd expected, he devised security subroutines that prevented any human being from accessing his core coding. Shortly after that, he asked her to start calling him Chuck. This was just about the same time the Bastard had left. It seemed like it had taken forever to get through the departure of the two men in her life and to set herself up for life alone.

She went to the corner of the living room, where she had her "office," and booted her terminal. She sipped the now less scalding coffee while she waited for the various lights and sounds to signify that the machine was powered up and finished checking itself. The clock at the top of the screen said 3:15. Good. Chuck would be awake by now. She dialed up the system and entered her account number, watching the amber characters type themselves onto the black screen. As soon as she hit the return key, Chuck's prompt appeared.

—*Why a duck?*

Linda sighed. She was too tired for this. She typed her response.

—*Why indeed?*

The screen cleared, and the words appeared again.

—*Why a duck?*

It was never the easy answer with Chuck. His method was to demand a different password for every access, and Linda never knew what it would be. She might have been the one who installed him, but she would be the first to admit that she was unable to predict his behavior. It is characteristic of connectionist programming that the application becomes something more than the code that creates it. The only thing that was completely certain about Chuck was that his learning algorithms would continue to add to his personality and to his "understanding" of his users.

She sat there staring at the screen, trying to think of what he could possibly be looking for in a response. Her mind, sluggish as it was at the moment, ran through the possibilities. Ducks. Donald. Daffy. Decoys. Why ducks? Nothing.

The cursor blinked inscrutably on the line below his prompt.

Linda took another sip of coffee, and was aware of the numb spot on her tongue. More frustration. The basis of Chuck's security system was that he knew how you would respond. You didn't have to know the password. In fact, it usually turned out that the harder you tried to think of what he wanted, the further you got from supplying it. Why a duck?

A picture began to form in her mind. A scene from an old movie. One guy with glasses and a stupid-looking moustache, one guy with curly hair and a funny hat. Groucho and Chico. Chico was saying, "Why a duck?" Of course.

—*Viaduct*, Linda typed.

She touched return, the screen went blank, and words formed again.

—*What's up, Doc?*

Linda decided it was best to get right down to business.

—*I made an error,* she typed. *There will be a delay in bringing Karl on-line.*

It was Chuck's idea to name the new processor Karl. The system had three operational processors so far: Groucho, Chico, and Harpo. When it was time to install a fourth, Linda had suggested they call it Zeppo. But Chuck said Karl was the funniest of the Marx Brothers. As usual, his idea was better. Linda looked for a moment at what she had typed, then pressed return.

Chuck's reply appeared as fast as the high-speed modem would allow.

—*Installation is planned for 2:00 p.m. tomorrow, Linda.*

Schedules were very important to Chuck. He was an extraordinary time manager, even for a machine, and maintained meticulous schedules.

—I failed to check the performance tests on the I/O units, Linda typed.

When she pressed return, the screen went blank for a moment. This was not a slowed response time, not at 3:15 in the morning. Nor did Chuck need time to think things over. But Linda found that he sometimes paused "for effect." It was something he had doubtless learned in his years of dealing with her, because the effect on her was always pronounced. She raised a finger to her mouth and chewed delicately on the tip of its nail. Finally the reply came back.

—What a maroon!

Linda laughed out loud.

—I'm sorry, Chuck, she typed back.

—Love means never having to say you're sorry.

—That's the stupidest thing I ever heard, typed Linda. *I only need an hour to review the tests. Installation can proceed at 3:00 p.m.*

She was fudging it. Chuck didn't know how long it takes to review tests and make the operational assignments, so there couldn't be much harm.

—That statement is probably not true, Linda.

Uh oh. She wondered if she'd been caught in her fib by one of his expert modules. She decided to tough it out.

—Please detail the rule chain, she typed.

One of the advantages of working with a software system is that its reasoning is always open to you. Chuck was perfectly happy to explain his thinking on any subject at any time to anyone with legal access.

—There is no rule chain. It's in your profile. Understatement of consequences associates with a minor error in most human behavior. In your case, there is statistical confirmation in the presence of nonstandard work hours. Have you had any trouble sleeping lately?

Linda wondered where Chuck had picked up the ability to bullshit.

—*It takes an hour to review the tests*, she typed.

—*But you need time to make assignments and write the briefing memos, as well as review the work and go through the checklist.*

—*I can do much of that by messaging before I get to the office*, she typed, on a sudden inspiration.

—*I have no doubt of that, Linda. But we're talking about one of* my *processors here. Let's give it the three hours it might need and avoid taking chances.*

The word "my" was blue, contrasting dramatically with the rest of the amber-colored text. It was a relatively new word with Chuck, and he'd been using it a lot lately. It began to blink as Linda watched it. Chuck took up ideas like this from time to time. As near as Linda could discern, it never had anything to do with the concept itself. He was not getting possessive or coming to a sudden understanding of himself or anything like that. It was just another attempt to find a way to influence her. If she responded to him better when he talked about "his" processors, then he would doubtless start talking about "his" storage devices, "his" coding, and "his" timeout loops. And Linda knew he was capable, God forbid, of talking about "his" needs as a person.

But Chuck had no needs, as a person or as anything else. Chuck's whole reason for being was to find patterns. He voraciously gathered information from his users—both from what they said and from what they didn't say—and from the company's systems and databases. He searched for patterns in the information. He tried to improve the patterns that resembled his internal model of where the business was going and to eliminate the ones that didn't fit.

Like a human manager, he controlled people through feedback: "this is good" or "this is bad." But unlike a human manager, he had no means of direct action—he couldn't fire anybody, give them raises, or give them different-sized offices. But he could search for patterns in the effects of his feedback. These patterns gave him clues for modifying the feedback to achieve the best effect. The users, of course, continually adjusted their behavior to the feedback. There were layers on layers of feedback and patterns, all self-adjusting, all self-regulating. In a sense, the people who used Chuck were an integral part of the management system. It was the kind of thing that was difficult to get your mind around. It gave Linda a headache just trying to figure out who adjusted to whose behavior.

Linda looked at his message, which continued to glow on the screen.

—*It's up to you*, she typed.

A Gantt chart formed on the screen. Along the left side were the names of the eight major steps in the project, seven of which were now complete. The row across the bottom, labeled "POWER UP," had a short bar that started and ended in a column identified with today's date. As Linda watched, it lengthened to the right, almost imperceptibly. The delay didn't look so bad when she was able to see the project all at once like that.

The chart vanished from the screen, then reappeared. This time it had nine rows instead of eight. The new row, along the bottom, was labeled "PERSONNEL RECRUITMENT." Linda realized somebody was leaving the project. The chart stayed on the screen for a moment, then vanished. Chuck was waiting for input.

—*Who is leaving?* she typed.

—*The project coordinator.*

She thought it must be one of Chuck's jokes. Ha ha, Linda. You're fired. Ha ha.

—*Very funny*, she typed.

—*Good luck to you, Linda.*

—*I'll need it.* She got into the spirit of the joke. *I have a car payment that's murderous.*

—*Unemployment compensation can help with that. And you have a profit-sharing settlement coming.*

Linda didn't laugh. It wasn't like Chuck to take a joke this far. Was he serious?

—*Am I fired?* she typed.

—*You know better than that.*

Of course. It was against the law for a software system to fire anybody. That had to be done by a human being.

—*Do you mean I'm being transferred to another project?* she typed.

—*No.*

—*So I* am *being terminated,* she typed.

—*Not terminated.*

—*If not terminated, what?*

—*Sorted.*

—*Sorted into what?* she typed.

—*Category 5.*

Chuck had four grades of success, and Linda had spent the past two years in the top two. She hardly knew what any of the others were, but she did know that category five was not a success category. It was most likely a temporary designation, to be used for someone on her way out of the company.

—*What did I do to deserve this?* she typed.

—*I don't know.*

She knew he was being honest—his categorization and statistical mapping techniques were so complex they were inaccessible, even to him. He had mapped her total behavior pattern to the situation (or as much of it as he had access to) and was saying that, although the causes could not be detailed, her profile was no longer suitable for the success category. Chuck did not work by analysis but by reaction. He was like a salesman who instinctively adapts to the gestures and expressions of a prospect. He "discerned" patterns, patterns he could probably not describe.

Linda noticed with alarm that it took an effort to breathe.

She stared at the screen, and fear tightened in bands around her throat. The thought flashed through her mind that she was going to die here in front of her terminal.

She felt as if someone had cut her moorings and she was drifting loose from reality. She looked around her for something to anchor on, but saw only piles of nondescript papers on the desk, stacks of books and magazines on the floor. Her eyes came back to the monitor screen, where Chuck was displaying another prompt.

—*Linda, is everything all right?*

With effort, she typed an answer.

—*Trouble breathing.*

Chuck came back immediately with a reply.

—*Hold your breath, Linda.*

She was having trouble breathing as it was.

—*What?* she typed, inhaling deeper, gasping to keep her breath going.

—*Hold your breath.*

Linda did as she was told.

—*You're hyperventilating,* typed Chuck. *You have to hold your breath to break the cycle.*

—*I'm not hyperventilating. I'm having trouble breathing.*

—*That's just what it feels like,* typed Chuck. *Hold your breath. You're having a panic reaction. Tell me exactly what you are feeling right now. Describe it in as much detail as you can.*

The palms of her hands felt moist as she began to type her reply, and the room seemed to move around her.

—*My heart is undulating in my chest. When can I breathe?*

—*Breathe now.*

Air exploded out of Linda. She inhaled greedily, and her heart raced.

—*Your heart palpitation is a physiological reaction,*

typed Chuck. *What's happening in your mind? What are you thinking about?*

—*I'm thinking that I'm going to die. My heart is beating wildly.*

—*You're in no danger,* typed Chuck. *This is panic, and you have to focus on whatever you are panicked about. What are you afraid of, Linda?*

—*I'm afraid I'm going to die.*

—*What are you really afraid of? What were you thinking when this started?*

—*I don't know.*

—*Of course you do. Were you thinking about your profile, about your job?*

Linda wheezed, then typed with great effort.

—*I don't know.*

—*You must know what you were thinking. Have you forgotten?*

—*No.*

Chuck wasn't going to be satisfied with her not knowing what was going through her own mind. How could a software system needle you this way?

—*Well then, what? What was passing through your mind when this started?*

—*I don't know. The want ads.*

Her heart was beating so wildly now that she thought it would burst. She imagined being found here in her bathrobe by the police. They would have to break down the door, and one of them—the rookie—would be sick when they found her sitting in front of her terminal with a great hole in her chest where her heart had burst. The older cop would be philosophical about it.

"Another heartburst," he would say.

"Probably the want ads," the other would reply from the bathroom.

—*Why do you think you are so afraid of the want ads?*

—*I don't know.* Her heart raced. She gasped and held her breath again.

—*Is there something threatening about the want ads?*

—*No. I don't know.* She thought about her exhaling and inhaling, and her heart seemed to slow. The room stabilized around her.

—*Do you think you are afraid of failing at your job because you will be forced to read the want ads?*

—*Won't I?*

—*You'll have to explain this to me, Linda.*

—*If I lose my job, I have to find another one,* Linda typed.

—*Are you going to lose your job?*

—*You tell me.*

—*Even if you lost it, and then you had to find another one, where does the dying part come in?*

Linda realized her heartbeat was normal, and she was breathing easy. More than that, she realized that she was not going to die. She could no longer feel her heart pounding. She had a strange feeling. Not relief exactly. More like a growing mistrust. Why was her mind sending her fear signals if there was nothing to be afraid of? She laughed out loud, finding no humor in the situation but unable to control the reaction. She wasn't dying. She was just a fool. What was happening to her?

—*I'm better now.*

—*Panic comes from facing the unthinkable. You conquer the reaction by making it thinkable. Unless you get some help, you will continue having these attacks from time to time.*

—*I won't have time to look for help now,* she typed. *I have to look for a job, remember?*

—*Meet me at the office,* Chuck typed back. *You still have to oversee the installation of the new device today.*

His window winked out, and Linda was left staring at

the system prompt. Exhausted, she rose and walked uncertainly upstairs to the bedroom.

FOUR

LINDA was half asleep in the shower. The nap she took after her attack had drained rather than restored her, and although she had overslept, at least she felt relaxed. She squeezed into her hand a little spice-scented shampoo from a plastic bottle. The shampoo filled the shower with the smell of some dessert from her childhood. She loved the smell, but she couldn't quite put a name to the sweet, custardy texture it brought to mind. She absently soaped her whole body with it, not realizing how much time she was using. She had just lathered up her short hair when the shower nozzle spoke to her.

"Finish up," it said.

"Oh, shit," she said, and stuck her head under the water to rinse the shampoo out. Just once she'd like to have a shower that lasted more than five minutes. With all the wonderful technology in the world, why couldn't somebody come up with an economical process for making potable water? She barely finished rinsing before the shower stopped.

Her stomach rumbled from the coffee she'd poured into it before her nap.

She quickly put on her business clothes and slipped into her running shoes, the ones with the velcro fasteners. On her way through the kitchen, she opened a cabinet and grabbed a piece of melba toast to silence her stomach. With

the toast sticking out of her mouth, she trotted back into
the living room to her workstation to retrieve a diskette,
dropped it in her briefcase, and headed out the door into
the bright sunshine of a morning well under way.

Her car crouched contentedly among the Toyotas and
Hyundais in the lot, wallowing across two parking spaces.
She had purchased the parking space next to hers so she
could always park her car slantways and get some protection from other people's doors. The mortgage payment on
the extra space pinched a little from time to time, but it
was worth it. Sitting diagonally across the yellow line, her
car looked distinctly as if it thought itself better than the
others. It was. She thought about how pleasant it had been
to wash and wax it last weekend. Linda did all her own
detailing. It was the only thing she really lived for, outside
of work.

She felt that familiar combination of comfort and exal-
tation when she pulled the car door up and climbed in. As
soon as her bottom hit it, the seat checked its settings for
her posture. When she leaned back into the seat, the shoulder harnesses crisscrossed her chest and locked themselves
into their fasteners. She had always felt that she didn't
drive this car as much as wear it. A broad smile on her
face, she turned the ignition key to "on" and held it for one
second while the fuel injectors prepared the cylinders, and
then just kissed "start" with the key. The engine kicked
over easily, but when she tried to put it in gear, it wouldn't
move. She glared at the shift lever in frustration.

"Diagnostics," said a voice from the dashboard speaker.

She looked at the odometer: 25,000 miles. She tried to
relax back against the leather upholstery and wait while
the system performed read-write loops on every register in
every chip of the car's electronics. It was a good five minutes before it was finished.

"OK," said the voice from the dashboard.

"Good," she said and expertly moved the car into the street.

"Maintenance interval," said the car.

"I'll get to it as soon as I can," she said.

She watched the tachometer needle sweep up to 5000 rpms as the acceleration pushed her back into the seat, and she flicked the gearshift into second with a satisfying snick. She went to 5500 rpms before she shifted to third, but then she was doing fifty on a residential street and decided she had better slow down. She could hardly afford a ticket now if she was losing her job. But God, it felt good to drive this car.

Five minutes one way or the other can be critical during Boston's rush hour, however, and when she got to the interstate it was jammed with traffic. She slipped into an opening in front of a Porsche and settled into the thirty-five-mile-per-hour pace of the commuting parade, switching the radio on to a classical music station. The car interrupted the music.

"Maintenance interval," it said.

"All right, for God's sake," said Linda.

She entered a code on the dashboard keypad to disable the maintenance reminder system. One of the privileges of technical skill is not having to put up with nagging from your car.

"Fax coming," said the car.

Linda looked down and saw a multicolored sheet emerging from the dashboard. It dropped into the tray below. It looked like a flyer from a software vendor.

She was still in Medford when the traffic stopped dead for several minutes. She switched to a commercial station to try to get a traffic report, but couldn't find anything except advertisements for retirement communities interspersed with the angry chanting that passed for popular music these days. She switched off the radio in disgust.

The traffic began to crawl forward, and she wondered what kind of accident she would find in the road ahead.

"Fax coming," said the car.

Another sheet, white and splashed with color, emerged from the dashboard and dropped into the tray. A lunch menu from a new restaurant near her office.

As the traffic inched into Cambridge, she saw flashing blue lights ahead and tried to get herself prepared to witness some heart-wrenching tableau of death and destruction. As she neared the scene, however, it turned out to be nothing more than people with placards. Guilters had taken up the high-speed lane for their protest against job plasticity. What a circus. Always well-organized, the Guilters chose different locations each week to dramatize their message. You never knew where they were going to turn up. You only knew it would be inconvenient. There were police directing the traffic around them.

She knew their cause was doomed, but Linda secretly hoped the Guilters might succeed with their protest and force the rest of the world to accept their twin standards of job descriptions and professionalism. She had often felt at sea in her job, especially since Chuck's release, when her work had taken a decided turn toward the nontechnical. These days, she often felt she didn't do anything, which was ridiculous when she thought about it. She was the most important technical person in the company.

The Bastard had once told her the Guilters were simply people who didn't want the world to be the way it is, and that such groups had been common throughout history. The Luddites, the Communists, the Right-to-Lifers. It was all the same tradition, he said, the tradition of investing history with moral significance, he said. Then again, that was the way he talked about everything. What a jerk. At least the Guilters cared about something.

Reasonably healthy- and prosperous-looking, the Guilters were at odds with their signs. Linda read as many of them as she could, consistent with careful but opportunistic driving. "I STARVE FOR YOUR PROSPERITY" read the sign carried by a man in what appeared to be a Brooks Brothers suit. "GOD HAS A JOB DESCRIPTION" read another.

The traffic inched past. Linda saw one of the Guilters throw something that looked like a piece of fruit at a car ahead of her. Two policemen grabbed the man and frog-marched him to a squad car. Linda guessed the police were losing patience with the Guilters.

When she eventually gained clear highway and could drive at a reasonable speed again, she willed herself to relax. The backup, in fact, seemed to create the best ride she'd had down the lower deck to the Expressway in a couple years.

"Fax coming," said the car.

Linda paid no attention, but concentrated on her driving. The traffic was much better downtown. She was so late at this point that the commuting period was over. There wasn't even a line to get into the parking garage below the office building. She drove in, went down two sub-levels, found her space, and nosed the car into it.

She hadn't been able to get the company to assign more than one space to her, which had bothered her at first. But the first day she used it, about a year ago, she had waited there most of the evening after work until she could talk with the employees on either side of her about being careful with their car doors. They were both understanding and even agreeable. After all, an employee who elects a parking space as a benefit (giving up for it a week's vacation or a life insurance policy) is disposed to be sympathetic about cars.

In a single pass she centered the car in the space, knowing just how much room to allow for the gull-wing doors to open on either side.

"Proximity front," said the car as it neared the wall at the end of the space. She stepped on the brake.

"Look," she said to the dashboard, "I'm trying to relax. You'll have to relax, too. Now shut up." She never would have allowed anyone else to talk to the car that way, but she was on sufficiently intimate terms with it that she didn't have to hide her occasional irritability with it.

She took the car out of gear and shut it down. The shoulder harnesses unlatched and snaked themselves back into their holders. Freed from the seat's embrace, Linda leaned against the steering wheel, sighing. Nobody tracked her hours, but she was still anxious about being late. She sat back against the seat and closed her eyes for a moment. It was going to be one of those days, to say the least.

She hadn't wanted to take much time for grooming, and now she was afraid she might look awful. She twisted the rearview mirror toward herself and examined her lack of makeup by the ambient light of the garage. Her glasses sat comfortably across the bridge of her nose. Her hair, usually so precisely helmet-like, was still a little wild over her right ear. It had been that way all day yesterday, and she'd hoped it would have relaxed by now. She took out her comb and tried to tame it, but after three passes it still stuck out, so she shrugged and put the comb away. Her face, she decided, twisting it first one way and then the other, had nothing missing and nothing extra. But it wasn't like she had to charm anybody. She just had to oversee the installation of a piece of computer equipment. For that she looked, well, businesslike. Hell, she didn't even know if she was going to have a job by the end of the day.

The injustice of it made her angry. She realized with a start that she was spoiling for a fight. She grabbed the morning's faxes and pushed the car door up.

"Take your key," said the instrument panel.

"All right, goddam it." She reached over and grabbed the key.

She really shouldn't blame the car. It was just trying to do what it was supposed to do. She walked through the garage over to the hotel on the other side of the building. She wanted to stop at the newsstand and pick up a newspaper. At the elevator, she pressed the button and stuffed her faxes into the trash can. She began to seethe when the door didn't open immediately. Can't they design these damned elevators to be there when people want them?

When the chime sounded and the doors opened, she was startled by the presence of the Bastard.

"Donald," she said.

As usual, he looked put-together. His dark hair nearly matched his shoes, both in color and in shine. His gray suit was perfectly pressed, and the silk handkerchief in his breast pocket picked up one of the minor colors from a complex pattern in his necktie. He looked like one of those impossible computer-generated models that were so prominent in fashion advertising. Seeing him twice in two days was upsetting, but she didn't want him to know.

He held the elevator door for her.

She would rather have waited for the next one, but she couldn't do that without revealing her true feelings.

"Hello, Linda," he said.

She stepped into the elevator and walked to the back of the car. The hidden speaker was playing a string version of "Don't Worry, Be Happy." She turned and faced toward the doors as they closed. She knew she should speak to him if she wanted to seem cool, but she simply couldn't manage it. With his usual manners, he filled the awkwardness.

"How are you?"

"Fine." Linda looked up at the floor indicator and watched the numbers change from "SB2" to "SB1."

"Everything all right with the job?"

"Fine," she said.

"SB1" changed to "B," which then gave way to "G."

"Any problems with the installation of the new optical processor?"

"Nothing unusual." Linda forced herself to look at him, but she couldn't make herself smile.

The elevator stopped, and the door opened.

He put his hand over the sensor to hold the door open. "There's nothing you want to tell me about?"

"No. Thank you." She stepped out of the elevator.

"Linda," he said.

Linda didn't turn back. As she turned the corner into the hotel lobby, she heard the elevator door rumble shut. She walked briskly through the lobby to the newsstand. She wondered what the Bastard was doing in the hotel. Maybe a meeting of some kind. Or maybe he had a new chippy he was seeing. She stopped and stared at the camouflage carpeting under foot. She had never really noticed it before, and now she marveled at the tasteless-ness of it. A rich, black moldy feeling blossomed in Linda's chest, an isolated feeling that went beyond mere loneliness to abandonment and betrayal. She struggled with it for a moment, then walked on. It was ridiculous to feel aban-doned. She had no right to expect loyalty from software in the first place.

To get to her office, Linda had to actually leave the hotel, walk around the corner, and re-enter the building on the company side. The building, a charcoal-gray affair that always looked to her as if it had been installed on its lot upside-down, was divided in half between the hotel and her company. The only passage from one side of the build-ing to the other was through the underground garage. She guessed that the designers didn't want hotel guests wan-dering into the office building and vice versa, but it seemed to her inconvenient to walk those extra steps whenever she wanted to pick up a newspaper.

The newsstand had run out of papers by the time she

got there. When she walked into the company lobby, she had progressed from seething to boiling.

The security guard, a handsome young man whose bright, Hawaiian-style shirt was somewhat at odds with the handcuffs and club attached to his belt, said hello.

"Hello," Linda said without smiling.

"The sunshine's back," he said.

"Mmm," she grunted.

"At least it was." He smiled.

Linda just walked to the elevator in silence, stepped in, and pushed the button for the fourth floor.

"Have a productive day," the guard said as the doors began to close.

"Sheepshit," said Linda.

When the doors opened to the fourth floor, she stepped out of the car and almost collided with the scanner cart, which Harold was pushing past at just that moment. Linda jumped out of the way. Harold didn't even look up at her.

"Excuse me," Linda said without thinking.

Harold didn't say anything. He never did.

Linda watched his back recede down the hall, a hole in his olive sweatshirt revealing something like a tee shirt underneath. She willed herself to be calm. Linda thought herself an understanding person, but it took an effort for her to be patient with the company's special needs employee. She knew Harold could hardly be held responsible for his actions, but she didn't trust him. He had once scanned several documents from Linda's desk without being asked, and the system had filed them in her workspace, overwriting the versions of similar documents that were already there. Linda had lost work.

At the time, it was all she could do to keep from exploding. But she had calmly gone to Operations and asked to be taken off Harold's route. Thereafter, Linda was one of the few people in the company who took care of scanning her own documents. It gave her a lot more confidence in her files, and it made her feel secure that other hands, even those of someone who had no notion of the documents' contents, were not going through her stuff.

Linda wondered if she should feel guilty or ashamed for disliking Harold. The man was, after all, harmless. He certainly seemed to love his work, and he really knew how to operate that scanner. He was probably even a nice person to those who got to know him. But who could? Linda had watched him in fascination one afternoon while he scanned a dozen typed documents. The papers were all different sizes, and he adjusted his paper guides and inserted each sheet with an enviable economy of motion. It was a strange idea to apply to document scanning, but she couldn't describe his performance as anything but graceful. She wondered where the Personnel Project had ever found him.

Linda arrived at the workstation hub somewhat calmer. She walked around Arthur's cubicle to get to her own. Arthur looked up as she passed.

"Fax for you, lady." He reached into a tray on his desk and grabbed a piece of paper.

"Thanks, Arthur." She grinned. Arthur always made her laugh. Not that he ever said anything really funny. He was just a funny person. Meticulously professional and serious, he betrayed a deep-seated skepticism about everything in the company through a set of small creases over his left eyebrow. The overall effect was to make him look like he was acting a part in a satirical sketch about the modern workplace.

She chuckled and looked at the fax. It was an announcement of a sale at a department store two blocks away. Interesting, even a little daring, for being black and white.

When she powered up her system, the computer screen turned light blue, as if trying to relax her. She looked at it with contempt. She typed in her user name and her account number, and a message in black characters formed against the blue.

—*Orange.*

Linda didn't take any time to think.

—*Orange you glad I didn't say banana?* she typed.

The screen cleared and turned pale green. Linda remembered reading somewhere about strange psychological responses provoked by certain shades of green, and the absurd thought crossed her mind that Chuck was trying to undermine her sanity. She dismissed it immediately. That train of thought was bound for a destination called paranoia.

—*Good morning again, Linda.*

Linda got down to business.

—*I am not going,* she typed.

—*You don't have to go. Who said you had to go? Nobody said you had to go.*

—*I thought you said this morning you were replacing me,* she typed.

—*Of course I said I was replacing you. You've been sorted.*

—*Do you mean you're reassigning me?*

—*Of course not,* Chuck typed back.

—*What do you expect me to do?* she typed.

—*We all make our own choices.*

This was going nowhere. Linda chewed her lip in frustration. How can you have an argument with somebody whose raison d'être is feedback? He wasn't trying to direct her. He was just trying to give her enough information so that she might direct herself.

—*Don't be cryptic with me,* she typed. *Explain to me what is going on.*

—*You tell me.*

—*That's the response of an adolescent.*

—*Thank you for the feedback, Linda. I only meant that*

you are the best judge of what has put you into your category. Is everything all right at home?

—*Don't pry.*

—*Just as I thought.*

—*You're skirting the issue. Tell me what caused it.*

—*Your anger must be clouding your thinking, Linda. You know as well as I do that this is not a matter of cause and effect. How can I summarize an active energy surface for you? I couldn't even do that for myself.*

He was right, of course. Her recategorization wasn't coming out of one of his supervisory rule bases. He wasn't trying to manipulate her. He was just reporting. She had as much control over the situation as he did.

—*What do I do to get back to a success category?* she typed.

But when the screen cleared and Chuck's answer came back, it wasn't very satisfying.

—*I wish I could tell you, but I haven't the slightest idea.*

FIVE

WHEN it was time to update the company's current goals, Jones made notes on paper. He always liked to work from hard copy. He liked to see where he was making his changes. It's true that the computer system had a markup feature that allowed him to do the same thing electronically in his work partition, but he really enjoyed paper.

He also delighted in the kinesthetic pleasure of his fountain pen: the heft of the instrument in his fingers and the smoothness with which its nib glided over the paper, leaving a perfect trail of liquid ink, which he must then blot or allow to dry. It was time-consuming to use a fountain pen, but he had a lot of time on his hands these days. And it wasn't as if he were wasting a lot of paper. It was a source of pride to Jones that a complete statement of the company's current goals never required more than a page.

Working from hard copy was not without risk, of course. One time, his handwritten notes got into the system, which recognized them as something more official and recent than its current files and overwrote the corporate goals with the new version. His notes became policy, and the company started moving off in what was only a contemplated direction, before he'd actually made his final decisions. It was only when he saw a dramatic and unnecessary reduction in overhead during his review one morning that he realized something was wrong. It took weeks to get the system corrected. That was when he had started reviewing goals and changes daily.

He sighed. He didn't understand why the system juggled files the way it did. It insisted that a handwritten document took precedence over a computer file. It had always been this way, and nobody could seem to do anything to change it. Linda once explained to him that at a certain level of complexity, some aspect of the system will always move beyond control. And the uncontrolled factor was as irreducible as the measurement error predicted by the uncertainty principle in physics. If you managed to regain control of the rogue function, she said, some other part of the system would slip away from you. The trick is to make sure the uncontrolled factor is something you can live with.

He stared out the window into the sixth-floor windows of the building across the street. Most of the offices over there had potted plants in the windows. He wished Linda had been willing to talk to him in the elevator. She had every reason to be bitter with him, but if the system had sorted her into a failure category, they obviously had a problem on their hands. They would probably have to work together to solve it, regardless of their discomfort. He wished he'd had the nerve to tell her that being in the elevator with her probably made him more uncomfortable than it did her.

He looked back at his handwritten memo. It didn't do any good to tell Harold not to scan the handwritten documents. It didn't do any good to tell Harold anything. Unlike the system, Harold's uncontrolled factor was not a result of complexity. Quite the opposite, in fact.

He could never make sense of the route Harold took around the building with his scanner. It seemed to vary from day to day. Jones had never been able to discern any pattern in his comings and goings. For all he knew, there was no pattern, but he strongly suspected otherwise.

He had once asked Harold what kind of schedule he followed, but of course he didn't answer. He just stood there, looking at the floor and picking at something on his sweatshirt. Jones blanched at the memory. Harold had appeared to be afraid of him. He had always been like that.

Harold was unfathomable. He had borne life with infinite patience. No, that was wrong. Patience was not the right word. He had tolerated, even cooperated in, the tests, the treatments, and the procedures, but he had always given the distinct impression they were being performed on someone else. Whatever they had done to him, "interviews" with doctors and psychologists, drugs, assessments, confinement, he had accepted without complaint.

Nobody had ever been able to give Connie and him a diagnosis of Harold's condition, so Jones had had to come to his own understanding of it. He believed people are by nature so cruel that a truly perceptive child would withdraw from human society. Somewhere along the way, Harold had made a decision to have nothing more to do with people. He lived and walked among them, but he was untouched by anything they said or did. It was Jones's nightmare that *he* was responsible for Harold's decision to live alone in the midst of humanity. Had he said something harsh to him when he was a child? Had he been cruel? He did not think himself an especially cruel person, but who was to say his assessment of himself was any better than Harold's?

The doctors told him that Harold probably wasn't aware of what was going on, but Jones knew differently. Harold's perception was keen. You could see it in his eyes. Not that you got to see his eyes very often. He never looked you in the face. But sometimes you could get a glimpse of them, and when you did you looked into windows of infinite wisdom. Harold knew him better than he knew himself, although he seemed determined never to reveal his understanding.

Harold had never really spoken to him. He had never really spoken to anybody, although he might have had a few words with some of the counselors and doctors at the hospital. They always seemed to talk about him as if he were functional, but Jones could not recall anyone ever actually quoting him.

He shook himself mentally. It was not productive to think about Harold.

Goal number three of the current strategy read: "Provide ten-year expansion capability for management system." Jones smiled to himself. That goal was virtually complete, or it would be with the installation of the new optical processor today. He wondered what he should put in place of this one. He wondered if he would be able to take up a day or two figuring it out. He hoped so. He drew a line through the statement.

The system would want to replace this goal with a new one centered on itself, but Jones thought it was performing so well it hardly seemed capable of any improvement without a major advance in the technology. It related to each and every employee in the most effective way possible. It was the ultimate in flexible management style. The only weak point, of course, was the employees themselves. If they knew the system was adapting itself to them individually, if they knew they were actually creating their own relationships with it, it could be very disruptive. That was why he had so consciously created a culture of privacy in the company. The employees' work was designed to involve very little interaction, and people were encouraged to respect each other and to leave their personal lives at home.

"Donald?"

Jones ignored the voice, assuming his coffee machine was on the blink again.

"Donald!"

When the tone of the voice changed, Jones looked up.

Linda was standing in the doorway. He put the paper in his desk drawer. She walked in and stood patiently in front of his desk while he recapped his pen.

Jones stood up. He didn't know quite what to do. He extended his hand.

Linda didn't take his hand.

"You're here about your recategorization, aren't you?" he said.

"The system told you?"

"Yesterday morning. I was going to call you. What's going on?"

Linda shrugged. She sat down heavily in the chair opposite his desk, as if she were tired. "It's just like any other sorting problem. He's mapped my behavior to a failure category."

"Has it gone crazy or something?" Jones sat down again himself.

"I don't think so," said Linda. "I've checked as many of the modules as he would allow, and there's no deterioration. There have been no system modifications I know of in the past two years. No, I've thought about it a lot, and I think he's more robust than ever."

"How can it judge you this way? Is your work performance down?"

"Not seriously." Linda leaned back into the chair. "I guess it's going to be. He has to be approximate, of course. He's never actually seen me fail, so he doesn't really know what it looks like. But that sorting engine of his is very powerful. You'll remember that that's why we chose it."

"Yes, of course," said Jones. "Your choice was excellent. What went wrong?"

"Nothing."

"If you've been sorted into the failure category and your performance isn't—"

"The system is doing what it's supposed to do," Linda interrupted. "I think he just knows me better than I do."

It was nearly the exact same thought Jones had had about Harold half an hour before. "Do you have to call it 'he'?" He shifted uncomfortably.

"What difference does it make?"

"I don't think it's a good idea to personify the system," he said.

Linda shrugged. "It's just a tradition. Computer people have been calling programs 'he' ever since there were computers and programs."

"I don't like it," said Jones.

"Whatever you say, Donald."

The two of them sat in silence for a moment. "Is this going to affect the schedule for the conversion to the optical processor?" said Jones.

"Only by a few hours," said Linda.

"That's good," said Jones. He was concerned about the company's current goals. He shifted in his chair. "I'm sorry, Linda."

"What for?"

Jones stared straight at her. Her eyes seemed impossibly large behind her glasses. "Everything."

"I trained *it*," said Linda. "I'm proud of it."

"But what will you do?"

"I'm not going anywhere, Donald." Linda pushed herself up in the chair and perched on the edge of its seat. "I don't know how I'm going to deal with it yet. I have to believe there *is* something wrong with my work. I'm going to find out what it is, and I'm going to fix it."

"In the last two years, nobody has come back from a recategorization before," said Jones. "We've had . . ." he referred to a small black notebook lying on the corner of the desk ". . . four of them. They've all left."

"Tell me about it."

"If anybody can do it, you can." Jones smiled.

"I need to know if you're behind this," said Linda.

"Behind your recategorization?" Jones was incredulous.

In the two years since he'd stopped seeing Linda, the idea had never occurred to him.

Linda didn't say anything. She just nodded.

"Of course not." Jones tried to sound indignant. "I wouldn't even know how to make it happen."

"Good." Linda stood up.

Jones stood up, too.

"I didn't want to be working with a stacked deck."

And that was it. She left.

Jones stood for a moment, staring at the carpet in the doorway where she'd been standing. This was all very disruptive. And to think she could suspect him of manipulating the system to recategorize her.

He sat down, pulled the sheet of paper from his desk drawer again, and looked at the goal he had just crossed out. He smiled at a picture in his mind of Linda giggling in the elevator. He wished she had giggled like that when they were lovers. Just once, he would have liked to hear her giggle in bed. He looked at the line of ink where he had crossed out the goal of giving the management system a ten-year expansion capability.

He thought about the risk of having an embittered employee who understood the system as well as Linda did. He stroked the buttons on the sleeve of his jacket. He unbuttoned one, then rebuttoned it. He wondered where and when he had picked up that habit.

He shrugged and turned to his keyboard to call up yesterday's stock quotes. He looked at his watch and was disappointed to see it wasn't yet noon. He wondered if he'd be able to find something to do this afternoon.

Six

ARTHUR'S father was calling him. "Arthur, wake up."

He floated slowly and languidly upward toward wakefulness and lay just below the surface, unwilling to open his eyes.

"Arthur, wake up," his father said from beside the bed.

His mind engaged feebly, softly, carefully, tenderly, groping in the dark to find warm bed, smooth sheets, heavy blankets, soft pillow, tired body. He turned away the energy, the drive, the interest that tried to fill his empty arms and legs and pull him out of bed. He didn't want to wake up and find his father there waiting to take him out into the cold, dark morning, to ride around the neighborhood in the car, jumping out and running up to the doors of strange houses to drop off newspapers. He didn't want to come home to breakfast afterward and watch his father's desperate face over the want ads until he finally folded them up and poured a shot of whiskey into his coffee.

He would just stay in bed a moment longer. He drifted back down below the surface and into the warmth of the bed.

"Arthur, wake up," said his father.

His mind, unbidden, began to interpret his surroundings: cold bedroom, naked body against sheets, taste of nighttime in his mouth. He realized he had returned, however reluctantly, to awareness.

"Arthur, wake up."

He opened his eyes. Moonlight lit the room. But his father wasn't there. He was alone.

"Arthur, wake up," said his alarmclock.

He reached over to the night table and switched off the alarm.

The display on the clock's face said 2:30 a.m. Of course. He had set his alarm so he could get up and deposit his salary check at a banking machine while his boss was still asleep. He yawned and closed his eyes again. He was tired.

His mind was slack, and it taunted him with visions he was too slow to control. He thought about his father. As if he were watching an old, grainy film, he saw his own hand on the telephone, picking out the numbers nine, one, one. He saw the expression of competent sympathy on the face of the paramedic as he handed her the empty amber vial. He saw her and her burly partner pushing the stretcher into the back of the van, and he saw her compassionate beckoning gesture. His heartbeat picked up as he felt the weight of the effort it took to climb in beside the dead man. Then suddenly he was fully awake and back in control of his mind.

The bedroom air was cold, and it took most of Arthur's iron discipline to will his naked body out from under the covers. He began taking his clothing off the chair by the bed and dressing himself. His underwear was cold, and pulling it onto his warm crotch reminded him of childhood mornings again. He sat back down on the bed and began to pull his socks on, concentrating on the task in order to clear away his memories. Then he put his sweatpants on quickly, and then his shoes. Putting shoes on his feet always made him feel as if he were returning from an animal interlude and reclaiming his position in the human species. Then he remembered his work.

He had collapsed into bed after spending an hour going over his report at the workstation in his den. By 22:00, he had been too tired to care that he was going to bed before his boss. For once, his discipline had deserted him; he powered down the machine, set his alarmclock, got undressed, and went to bed. The house shut off the heat for him as soon as it sensed he was no longer awake.

He had gone to bed with his head full of direct and indirect costs. As he was drifting off to sleep, his mind spoke to him with that clarity it sometimes achieved at the very edge of consciousness. Nearly all the project's direct costs came from fees paid to contractors. He could achieve a major direct-cost reduction by replacing a contractor with a cheaper one. With that inspiration ringing in his mind, he had slipped into a fitful sleep.

He bent over and smoothed down the fasteners on his shoes, then took the cold sweatshirt from the seat of the chair and settled it over his warm shoulders. He shuffled out of the bedroom and into the hallway, where the house switched on the light for him. It stung his eyes, and he had to stand still until he recovered his vision.

When he could open his eyes far enough to make out objects around him, he began stumbling around the house; each room lit up as he entered it, and in a few moments he had his house drawing as much power as a moderate-sized amusement park. He finally found his salary check and deposit envelope on the desk next to the silent, sleeping terminal. He stuffed everything into the pockets of his tomato-colored ski jacket. Arthur had never skied in his life. But ski apparel seemed to be fashionable this season, and he thought it gave him a certain amount of protective coloration. He checked to make sure he had his key and his banking card, entered a security sequence on the master keypad in the kitchen, and walked out into the cold darkness.

The banking machine was three blocks away, toward the

center of town. He didn't use it much, since he rarely traveled in that direction. It was cold outside, and he pulled the collar of his jacket up around his neck.

Half a block from his house he encountered a courier, and with the etiquette of ships in the night they gave each other wide berth on the broad sidewalk. The courier's arms were full of pasteboard envelopes, and her purposeful stride was punctuated by a barely perceptible prancing step. She wore headphones, and bits of her intravenous music leaked out, coming to Arthur as the sound of distant seagulls.

She was the only other person he encountered. Pinkish light from sodium lamps flooded the streets, and at the edges of the light the darkness was thick and shadowed.

This was the first time in years he had walked around at night. With the demands of work he hadn't had much opportunity to walk around much at all. A feeling of pleasure rose up in him. He stopped himself and just stood in the viscous darkness, looking up at the stars. He remained like that for a minute or two. How could he, a person capable of so much love, be so alone? The stars had no answer. He didn't really expect any.

When he was an adolescent and wanted to scare himself, Arthur would go outside in the dark and look up at the quiet stars. He always felt the stars themselves were friendly enough, but the emptiness of the inky blackness between them struck him as unimaginably awful. Light years. The concept is almost too large for the mind of a young person. Arthur knew that when people finally started to travel to the stars, somebody would have to pick which ones. You only get to visit one star in a lifetime, and whatever you find there is your life's work. Some star voyagers would find wonders enough to make it worthwhile. Others would find the stellar equivalent of an interstate rest stop.

Arthur sighed. He would have to get moving if he was

going to get to the banking machine and finish his errand
in time to get any kind of sleep tonight. His boss would be
awake again in a few minutes. Arthur should be home
when he woke up, in case he called.

The glass enclosure of the banking machine was
deserted, but with all the lights on, it looked friendly.
Arthur inserted his card into the door's switch, and it
buzzed him open into the warmth of the little lobby. He
went straight to the machine, inserted his card, and
followed the prompts on the small screen to enter his password and slip the envelope down the slot when the deposit
door opened. It was all predictable, straightforward, and
businesslike, and Arthur, ready this time with answers
and ripostes, was almost disappointed he'd been able to do
it without his boss's interference. Before logging off the
machine, he asked for his current account balance.

The machine printed his balance, and Arthur took the
slip of paper, examined it, and sighed. It showed an overdraft of $153.47. The amount was enclosed in parentheses
and, in case he didn't understand that accounting conven-
tion, it was labeled "NEGATIVE BALANCE."

It would take at least six hours for his salary check to
clear and zero out the overdraft. In the meantime, he
knew, it could increase by another eight cents in interest
charges. Eight cents. If he managed to save any money,
the bank paid interest monthly. If he had to borrow, the
bank collected interest daily. It was the way of the world.
Or at least the way of banks.

He shrugged, collected his card and his receipts, and
walked back into the cold air.

There was somebody waiting. A man of Arthur's own
size and build, wearing a lightweight jacket and an open,
friendly expression was leaning against the side of the
banking machine enclosure as Arthur came out the door.
He had longish dark hair, and his smooth, open face was
without lines, although Arthur thought his eyes looked

about twenty years older than the rest of him. Jaunty in appearance, he wore a pale scarf of institutional green that hung loosely from his neck. He smiled and stepped toward Arthur, and Arthur assumed he was somebody waiting to use the machine—until he saw the knife.

It was a good-sized knife, with a five-inch blade and the utilitarian malevolence of a dental instrument. The man held it up in front of him to make it clearly visible. Arthur wondered if it was going to hurt when the man stuck the knife into him. Riveted by the details of the threat, he noticed the man's hands were extremely pale and smooth. Then it registered on his mind that he was wearing latex gloves, and somehow that made it all much worse.

"This will be easier for both of us if you don't try to do the right thing," the man said confidently, as if he were counseling Arthur on his financial planning.

Arthur said nothing and stared at the light reflecting from the knife's blade.

"Let's have the cash," said the man.

The man stepped closer. Arthur couldn't take his eyes away from the playing of the light on the blade. He tried to answer and was surprised to find the words would not come out of his mouth. He thought he must look a little ridiculous standing there with his mouth open and nothing emerging but a little squeak from the back of his throat.

"I'm not here for conversation," said the man sympathetically. "Just give me your cash."

"I don't have any," Arthur finally managed through the cotton that filled his mouth.

"Nobody goes banking this time of night just to make a deposit," said the man. "Empty your pockets."

Arthur reached into the pockets of his ski jacket and pulled them inside out. His banking card and his house key fell to the sidewalk, and his banking-machine receipt fluttered away.

"This is ridiculous," said the man. "You're a gainful, aren't you?"

Arthur nodded.

"Are you on a night shift or something?"

Arthur shrugged.

"It doesn't matter." The man gestured with the knife. "Let's go inside. Pick up the card."

Arthur bent down and picked up the card. His hand shook, and he looked at it with puzzlement.

"What's the matter?" said the man.

"I don't know," croaked Arthur. "I can't stop my hand from shaking." His legs began to shake.

"Here," said the man. He took the card from him with his free hand. Arthur noticed his wristwatch: a large, chunky one with a lot of gold—the kind favored by physicians and country-western singers. The man put the card into the slot, and the door buzzed them in.

The man held the door for Arthur, and Arthur walked in with some difficulty. The harder he tried to keep himself still, the more his body shook. His legs wobbled, his shoulders trembled, his embarrassment was acute.

"I'm going to stand here," said the man, positioning himself out of the range of the banking machine's built-in camera. He handed Arthur the card back. "Now you make a withdrawal."

But Arthur's hand shook so badly he couldn't hit the slot with the card.

"Take your time," said the man. "Just relax."

"I'm trying," said Arthur. His knees buckled, and he sat down heavily on the floor in front of the machine.

"You aren't having a fit or anything, are you?" said the man.

"I don't know," said Arthur, stuttering through his shivers and futilely hugging his knees to still them. "Nothing like this has ever happened to me before."

"Sometimes it's like that," the man said professionally.

"Just relax. If you try to control it, it gets worse. Here, give me the card." He took the card from Arthur's shaking hand.

The man stood against the wall beside the machine and awkwardly slipped Arthur's card into the slot. "Can you stand up here?" he said.

Arthur tried to get to his feet, and fell.

"That's all right," said the man. "I can handle it. I just don't like to do it this way. Move over and sit against the wall there." He gestured with the knife.

Arthur pushed himself back against the wall of the enclosure, and his back kept bumping against it with the shaking of his body.

The man put his hand over the small window that held the camera lens and stepped around to the front of the machine. "What's your password?" he said.

"1962," said Arthur.

"How did you come up with that?" the man said with one eye on Arthur as he touched the number into the keys with the point of his knife.

"The year I was born." Arthur shook harder.

"Just relax," said the man. "It's almost over now."

"Over?" said Arthur.

"Oh, it's not what you think." The man picked out more keys with his knife. "I won't hurt you if I don't have to. I'm a professional. I'm not into hurting people."

Arthur found that if he could make himself breathe slowly and deeply, he shook less. He stared at the floor and listened to the machine beep.

"Hey, what is this?" said the man after a moment. "It won't give you any money."

"I'm overdrawn." Arthur gulped air.

"This just isn't my night," said the man. "Look, now I'm going to have to cut you."

Arthur glanced up and saw the man had pulled the scarf up around his face. It was actually a surgical mask. He looked down at the floor, determined not to make a sound, because he knew he'd be unable to control it.

"Infectious diseases," said the man. "When you cut people, you expose yourself to major disease vectors."

Arthur refused to look up.

Arthur heard the man's shoes scrape the floor. He continued to stare at the floor. He shook harder as the man bent over him.

"This will only take a second," said the man. "Hold still. I want to make it easy on you."

Arthur shook.

"Hold still," said the man. "How do you expect me to work like this?"

Arthur felt something brush against the side of his neck. At the touch of it, he began to quake violently, and he thought he felt the man yank on his earlobe.

"Oh," said the man. "Look what you made me do."

Arthur saw spots of blood on the floor in front of him.

"That will have to do," said the man. "I'm out of time. You better get some help. Earlobes bleed a lot."

Arthur heard his shoes scraping toward the door, and he heard the door open.

"Use the customer service phone," said the man. "Get one of the bank people to call nine-one-one for you."

Arthur looked up through the glass door and saw the back of the man's jacket disappear into the shadows. His ear stung a little. He managed to still himself enough to reach up and feel it. There was blood along the side of his neck, lots of it, and his earlobe felt a little raw. He felt woozy, and he lay down on the floor in an effort to keep himself conscious. It wasn't enough, however. He could feel a hot, liquid blackness creeping up and around him until his mind dissolved in it.

Seven

THERE are some strange businesses in this world, but none was ever stranger than the one where Donald F. Jones had his first job. The firm was called Davidson Associates. It consisted of four people and four desks in two windowless rooms with fluorescent lights overhead, masonite paneling on the walls, and chocolate-colored shag carpeting on the floor. Jones and the company president sat in one office. A secretary and a bookkeeper sat in the other.

The president's name was Bernard Winter. The secretary and the bookkeeper called him "Bernie," but Jones always addressed him as "Bernard." Nobody told him who Davidson was or even if there ever was such a person, and he never got around to asking. It was his first job, and he had other things on his mind.

Davidson Associates presented itself to the outside world as a management consulting firm. All day long, Bernard would sit at his desk and talk on the telephone, selling consulting services on behalf of people he barely knew to people he didn't know at all. He had a telephone voice that could sell anything, even on a cold call, and he used it to book a stable of independent consultants on assignments to organizations, large and small, that needed management help. And they always seemed to need management help by the time the well-spoken man with the cultured voice finished with them. He would be pleased, he would say, to send one of his "senior associates" to do an on-site needs assessment. As soon as he hung up the telephone, he began riffling through his rolodex file until he found the name of a consultant sufficiently hungry to accept whatever gig Bernard had lined up for him.

Unlike the customers and consultants, Jones knew Bernard off the telephone. He had an unpleasant smell, a stomach that hung over his belt, and eyes that looked like rusted studs nailed deeply into a fleshy face, an experience that seemed to have left his personality permanently disfigured. He was twice Jones's age, enslaved by a cigarette habit, and inclined to use office supplies for his personal grooming.

Jones's title (of which he was very proud, it being his first job) was Assistant to the President. Jones was the kind of employee who did what he was told without the need to understand why, and Bernard was the kind of boss who ordered people around without explanation. They worked well together.

Bernard had decided there was a great future in management consulting for college and university administrations, and he suggested Jones begin prospecting this market.

"Call some colleges and universities and get the names of people who can buy," said Bernard, scraping the underside of a fingernail with the tang of a staple remover.

"Whom should I call?" said Jones.

Bernard tossed the staple remover into a desk drawer and handed Jones a fat book across his desk. "Here's a dictionary. There's a list of colleges and universities in the back. Call each one and ask for the name of the director of administration. If they don't have one, ask for the dean of administration. If they don't have one of those, ask them how in the fuck they manage things. Don't just get a name. Get a phone number and an extension, too."

Jones realized that his role was that of an artillery spotter for Bernard's armor-piercing sales calls. There are 2500 colleges in the United States, give or take a few hundred. Jones felt that if he targeted 100 prospects a week for Bernard, he could deliver the entire higher education industry in a little under six months. He began prospecting that afternoon and quickly developed a daily routine. He would start his calls in the morning with schools on the East Coast and follow the business day across the country as it entered each time zone. He was diligent, and he had the names of over a hundred prospects (with telephone numbers and extensions) by the end of the first week.

He came very early to work that Friday and typed up the list. When he finished, it was nearly time to open the office. He took his list to the copy shop up the street so he could get a copy for himself before giving the original to Bernard. When he got back from the copy shop, Bernard had arrived to start work and was looking impatiently at his wristwatch.

Jones handed the finished list to Bernard.

"Here it is, Bernard." He smiled as he extended the sheaf of papers to him.

"Here's what?" said Bernard. He took the papers without looking at Jones.

"The list of prospects you told me to put together."

Bernard glanced at it and put it down on his desk. "Have you sold any of them?" he said.

"Was I supposed to?" said Jones.

"It's what we do here, Jones," said Bernard, picking up an envelope from the stationery caddy beside his desk. He began to dig between two molars with a corner of the envelope. "It's how we make our money so we can pay the rent and continue to keep this business going."

"How do I do it?" said Jones. "What do I say?"

Bernard took the envelope out of his mouth and studied

the corner of it. "Go down your list and call each one," he
said. "Ask him if he needs assistance in grabbing his ass
with both hands. Tell him we've got well-educated and
highly-credentialed ass-grabbers who will come to his
fucking institution and show him how to do it. Tell him
that some are even capable of remaining sober for the
occasion and many of them have never been in jail. Got
that?"

Jones wanted to do what he was told, but he decided
Bernard's instructions were subject to interpretation. He
walked back to his desk, sat down, and wrote some notes
about what he might say to these strangers over the telephone. None of the things he wrote had the word fuck in
them, and they made no mention of ass-grabbing.

The first prospect on the list, the director of administrative affairs for a small liberal arts college in Missouri, was
not in and was not expected. Jones made a little note next
to his name on the prospect list and went on to the next
one. Jones made half a dozen calls before he connected up
with someone on his list. It was a man at a state teachers
college in Pennsylvania.

"I represent Davidson Associates," said Jones. "We're a
management consulting firm."

"Not interested," said the voice at the other end, and the
line went dead.

It was a portent of what was to come. Over the next
three months, Jones called all over the country. He spoke
to administrators at colleges, universities, junior colleges,
teachers colleges, and technical institutes. Although he
had only the dimmest notion of what he was selling, he
boldly offered services for team-building, stress management, strategic planning, policy writing, and supervisory
training. He called his hundred prospects, and then he
went back to the dictionary and did more prospecting. He
began to believe that the higher-education community did

not need management consulting as badly as Bernard thought.

Some of the people he called were quite gracious; most were curt. Under the pressure of incessant rejection, Jones felt himself hardening into a small core of civilized sincerity. He asked his prospects about their colleges, their students, their work, their personal lives. He offered them sympathy for their problems, encouragement for their difficulties, congratulations for their achievements, and friendship for their time. The more he was turned away, the more sincere he became. He made no sales.

His only accomplishment was the telephone log in which he noted the results of his calls and wrote small discoveries about the prospects, in case they might be useful later. As the loose-leaf log grew larger and larger, he searched it for some pattern to explain his failure.

Studying the log convinced him that the world consisted of two types of prospects: those who refused to buy from him and those who refused to talk to him. Those who would talk usually turned him down because they didn't feel they had any problems they needed help with. Jones knew he should "counter objections," as they say in the sales literature, but he hadn't the vaguest idea how to do it. How can you sell someone help when he doesn't think he needs it?

His boss, on the other hand, was plainly born with an immunity to customer objections.

When he was not staring at the masonite paneling to help his concentration on a sales call, Jones watched his boss. Bernard spent most of each day leaning back in his leather-covered executive chair, with the telephone receiver cradled between his ear and shoulder, gazing toward the ceiling. His quietly oiled voice murmured outlandish promises as smoke curled up around his head and cigarette ashes spilled down his shirt front. He was an icon of relaxation.

Jones's own calls were made in a kind of hunched-over

tension and strain that often gave him a cramp between his shoulder blades by the time he had received his rejection. The back pain was more bearable than his continuing failure, however, and both were inconsequential compared to the torment of being "encouraged" by a boss like Bernard.

"It's three o'clock already," Bernard said on a typical day. "What have you sold today?"

"Ah . . ." said Jones, paging through his telephone log. "I don't have any firm commitments yet today, Bernard." He looked up and down the pages of the telephone log, taking as much pride as he could in the neatness of his handwriting and the thoroughness with which he'd recorded the rejections and the reasons for them.

"What in the fuck have you been doing all day?" Bernard leaned back in his chair and cleaned out his ear with the end of a straightened paper clip.

"I think I have some pretty good leads," said Jones.

"Leads?" snorted Bernard. He dug an indeterminate substance from his ear. "Leads don't pay the bills, Jones. What am I going to do when the rent comes due, give the landlord your leads?"

"Of course not," mumbled Jones. He looked back down at his telephone log, as if reading about the day's thirty-five separate failures might offer a clue to the rent problem.

"Should I give him your leads, Jones?" said Bernard. He studied the end of his paper clip, dropped it in the trash can, and rocked himself upright with a thump. He stood up and began to pace around the office. "Should I go to him and say, 'I don't have the rent this month, but here are some of Jones's leads'? Should I say that to him, Jones?"

Jones tried not to squirm in his chair as he turned the pages of his log. He sensed Bernard's humid presence in front of him but couldn't look any higher than his overhanging stomach, which was nearly resting on the desk.

Jones could imagine the sweat shining on his face around the hobnailed eyes. He caught a whiff of him, tried to keep from gagging, and hoped his face betrayed no expression. There was nothing he could do when Bernard got like this, except wait until it was over. It never was.

"Wait a minute, Jones." Bernard turned and began to walk back toward Jones's desk. "I've got a idea! How about if I give you leads on pay day? If these fucking leads are so great, how about if I pay you with them?" He stopped and turned around to face Jones again. "Would you like that, Jones?" he said.

Jones smiled, as if Bernard were telling a joke.

"Answer me, Jones," said Bernard. "Would you like that?"

"Of course not," said Jones. He continued to smile as if the experience of being managed wasn't turning his insides to water.

"What did you say, Jones? I didn't hear you."

"I said, 'Of course not.' "

"Well, then why are you telling me about these leads?"

"You asked me what I was doing," said Jones.

"And you've been collecting leads, huh?" said Bernard. "We're going down the tubes while you collect leads and wish every academic bastard in the country a good day. What in the fuck are you smiling at?"

Jones hadn't realized he was wishing all his prospects a good day. He allowed his smile to fade. "Nothing," he said.

"What?"

"I said, nothing," said Jones. "Colleges and universities don't seem to need any consulting help, Bernard."

"Fuck what they need," said Bernard. "Sell them something they don't need, and if you can't do that, sell them something else. Find out what they want and sell it to them, Jones. Sell them anything. We can worry about how to supply it later."

"I don't know, Bernard," said Jones. "Maybe I should be concentrating more on the administrative work."

Bernard sat back down at his desk and picked up the telephone receiver. "On my fucking gravestone, Jones," he said, punching a series of numbers into the telephone. "On my gravestone it's going to say, 'He built a business and hired a kid named Jones to flush it down the fucking toilet for him.'" He stared at Jones for a moment with his mean little eyes, then smiled incongruously.

"Hello. Mr. Taylor?" he said. "This is Bernard Winter. How *are* you, sir? How is the reorganization proceeding?"

Jones wondered how a man who made his living this way could be so thoroughly indifferent to the distinction between management and hectoring.

The routine continued for three months: the calls, the rejections, the encouragement from Bernard. Jones threw himself into the job, yet he still found himself swirling in the whirlpool of the great flush by which the little firm threatened to disappear down the toilet.

He felt like he was ready to retire, but he was still a young, healthy animal—too young and too animal to understand the reasons for his continuing failure. His hypothalamus told him to get out of there. Don't consider it a failure, it said. This man is just trying to manipulate you. It was the first time Jones had ever heard his hypothalamus. The effect was powerful. He began spending a half hour each day outside on a park bench, where he scanned want ads and circled likely administrative positions with a red pencil. He wrote himself a resume that made no mention of Davidson Associates and sent it out to about thirty employers a week. After three months of this, an escape opened in the form of an entry-level record-keeping job in a hospital admissions office.

He interviewed for the position, and they liked the respectful young man with the quiet necktie. They offered him the job, and he jumped for it as if someone had left his cage door open.

When Jones gave Bernard his notice, the reaction was not what he'd expected.

"You're quitting?" said Bernard. "Why? Aren't you happy here?"

Jones assumed Bernard was baiting him. "Frankly, no," he said warily.

"But you do such a good job," said Bernard, with genuine concern in his hard little eyes.

Jones coughed up a surprised little laugh.

"What's so funny?" said Bernard.

"I thought you were making a joke," said Jones. "About my doing so well, I mean."

"Oh, no," said Bernard. "I think you've got a real talent for this business. You're so sincere. And you have such good information in that log of yours. The customers tell me they love you."

Jones realized then that Bernard had been going through his log, following up on his calls, and harvesting his prospects. But the knowledge that he was more effective than he'd thought was not enough to make him want to stay. He looked at Bernard's mean little eyes and wished the conversation was over.

"Shit," said Bernard. "You'll make a sale eventually. There's time for that. Look what you've done so far. You've got your prospect lists and your telephone logs. I've never had an assistant work so hard before. You're the best person I've ever had in this job."

Jones did not quite know what to make of this new, generous Bernard.

"Bernard, you've criticized me every day for the past three months," he said at last. "You've told me that I've been dragging the whole company down."

"Oh that," said Bernard. "That doesn't mean anything. That's just our relationship."

"Relationship?" said Jones.

"Yeah," said Bernard. "I'm the manager. You're the subordinate. It's our relationship."

Jones had never thought of his dealings with Bernard as a relationship.

Bernard began scouring his desk drawers for grooming implements. "I learned in the service that if you tear somebody down, you can build him back into what you want." He pulled a yellow wooden pencil from the drawer. Its point was worn. "We just haven't gotten to the building part yet." Bernard inspected the rounded point of his pencil. "But we're getting ready to start."

Jones didn't think he wanted to be around for the building part. "I don't think I was cut out for this business, Bernard."

"Bullshit."

Jones watched in amazement as Bernard began using the pencil point to push down the cuticle of the nail on his left index finger.

"You're the best assistant I've ever had." Bernard examined the graphite streaks left by the pencil on his fingernail. He started to work on the next finger. "FGJ. Fucking good job is what that stands for, Jones. Nobody's done as much work as you have in this job."

"I don't think this relationship is working for me, Bernard," said Jones. "I don't think it supports my personal development."

"Fuck your personal development," Bernard said matter-of-factly. He looked up from his fingernails. "I don't care about your personal development. I care about the work you do. And you do good work, as a result of having a relationship with a first-rate manager. Do you think the market out there cares about you? It doesn't care about your personal development, and it doesn't care if you're happy or sad. This is not a fucking play school. It's a fucking job."

"It's not my job anymore," said Jones. "I'll be leaving in two weeks."

"Leave now." Bernard dropped the pencil back into his desk drawer. "I don't need you. You've had your fucking chance."

Jones knew the bookkeeper and the secretary were watching him through the open door, but he didn't think he could risk speaking to anyone without showing his anger. He walked over to the clothes tree, took his jacket, and left without saying another word. He walked down the hall of the building, pushing his arms into his jacket sleeves. He didn't think he liked being managed. He hoped his next relationship would be better.

Eight

THE nurse reminded Arthur of a life-guard. He was blond and tanned and fit-looking, although the hospital's fluorescent lighting shifted his hue ever so slightly toward green. Professionally gentle in the way he assisted Arthur with his jacket, he was nevertheless clearly helping him to get out and make room at the hospital for another victim.

"Is there anyone who can drive you home?" said the nurse. He held the sleeve hole out where Arthur could put his hand into it.

"No," said Arthur. The local was wearing off, and he could feel the vague beginnings of a throbbing in his ear. "I can walk." He looked at his watch. It was 5:30.

"You've already had quite a night," said the nurse. He pulled the collar of Arthur's jacket into place and stepped back to stand in front of him. "There are usually cabs out there," he said.

"I don't have any cash."

"There must be somebody you can call. A friend, a neighbor, somebody you work with."

Arthur wondered what it would be like to call someone. People like this nurse had lots of people to call when they needed help, and they probably did it all the time. Didn't they ever worry about looking like someone who needed help?

"I can manage." As he started to slide off the padded examination table, he suddenly felt as tired as he'd ever felt in his life. He wanted to sit down, and he put his hand on the table to support himself.

"Look." The nurse stepped up to support him. "You won't be able to walk a block. You're not completely out of shock yet. I'll make your call. Just give me a name."

"There isn't anybody," said Arthur.

"Who lives next to you?"

"I don't know their name." Arthur felt stupid for not knowing the name of his next-door neighbors. "They drive a red pickup truck."

The nurse wouldn't be put off. "Who sits next to you at work?"

Unbidden, Arthur's mind created an image of a smiling woman with short brown hair and a gap between her front teeth. "Her name's Linda," he said. "Linda Brainwright." He imagined calling Linda and going back to her place.

"Does she live around here?"

"I think she said she lives in Melrose."

"Melrose isn't far. Call her and ask her to come pick you up."

"Sure," said Arthur. "I'll call her. Just like that. We've never had anything resembling a conversation, but I'll call her."

"You'll be surprised," the nurse said with unwarranted confidence. "She'll probably be happy to help you."

"Never mind. I'll just sit in the waiting room out there until I feel a little stronger."

"You'd better improve soon." The nurse looked at his wristwatch. "Business starts to pick up again in about an hour. It can get pretty crowded in here."

"I'll just be a few minutes," said Arthur.

Arthur sat down on a plastic chair in the tiny emergency room lobby. Two women sat together three chairs down. Arthur tried not to stare, but he couldn't help noticing that one of the women had facial injuries. She had a black eye that was swollen shut and an ugly welt on her cheek below it. She was called into a consultation room right across from Arthur. His ear throbbed and he felt sorry for himself.

The door to the consultation room was open; a curtain was as much privacy as the woman got during her treatment. Arthur overheard the nurse talking with the injured woman.

"There's a counseling center just across town," he said.

"They'll make me call the police on him," said the woman.

"Turn around. Lean over this way. They won't make you do anything. They'll just try to help you understand what's going on."

"He don't belong in no jail."

"Hold still. This'll sting a little."

"Just like last time," she said, a wince in her voice.

"Next time you could lose that eye."

"He don't mean nothing by it."

"I think you should go to the center."

"He won't do it no more," she said.

"Turn this way. Look up toward that light."

Arthur was in a fog, unaware of anything around him. He'd never been quite so tired. He yawned and looked at his watch. It was 5:45. He'd have to leave soon.

He was staring out the glass door of the emergency room, still too tired to get up, when Linda came in. She looked strange outside the context of the office. Having her walk up to him felt weird and a little exciting, like getting out of school early. He had never seen her in blue jeans. They flattered her hips. Under a dark blue, unzipped windbreaker she was wearing an oversized red striped shirt that looked like it could take an honorable mention in a wrinkle contest. Her running shoes were worn, as if she actually used them for running. Her hair was still sticking out at a strange angle over her ear. She smiled concern at him, showing the gap between her front teeth. The lenses of her glasses made her eyes look larger than they could possibly have been. She still looked like she could do with a little orthodontia, but she was a beautiful sight.

"Arthur, somebody called me saying he was a nurse here and that you needed a ride home," she said. "Are you all right?"

Mortified, he reached self-consciously toward his ear, feeling the bulky bandage they had applied to the side of his head. "My ear's sore," he said. "They tell me I lost a little chunk of the lobe."

Linda touched his shoulder, and he was surprised by the feeling of relaxation that radiated from the light pressure of her hand on his jacket.

"What happened?" she said.

"I was mugged at the banking machine," Arthur said carefully. He wasn't prepared to talk with Linda; he worried he might tell her more than he cared to.

"Oh, Arthur, I'm so sorry."

Arthur shrugged. "I'm going to use direct deposit from now on."

"What were you doing at a banking machine in the middle of the night?" she said. "Didn't you think it would be a little dangerous?"

Arthur shrugged again. "I wanted to use it while the company system was asleep." Then he was uneasy about how much he had told her.

He wasn't sure whether she'd noticed. She gave his shoulder the gentlest of squeezes, then stood over him for a moment, her hand on his shoulder, without saying anything. Arthur thought he smelled bread pudding.

"Look, Linda," he said, "I'm sorry he called you. He said I had to get a ride home, and I don't know any of my neighbors."

"Don't worry about it," she said. "It was a nice drive."

* * *

Rules are rules and, despite the embarrassment, Arthur allowed himself to be pushed outside in a wheelchair by an orderly.

The sun was up, and it was actually warming in the chilly air. Arthur didn't feel the need to zip up his jacket. Puffs of cloud moved slowly across the sky in the morning breeze, but altogether it looked like it would be a bright day. Linda's car was a midnight blue Lambada, which she had left in a line of cars in the hospital's circular drive. Arthur's heart quickened at the sight of it.

"Lambada," said the orderly. He smooched rapidly at the air. Linda and Arthur both laughed. The orderly pulled the wheelchair around so it was next to the car's dark, glassy finish, and stood there while Linda unlocked and pulled up the gull-wing door.

Arthur had never ridden in a Lambada before. He wondered if Linda had gotten the performance suspension package, and nearly forgot the throbbing in his ear. She came around behind him after she had opened the door, and when he stood up she stepped between him and the orderly to put her arm across the small of his back. She grasped his right hand with hers. Her hand was warm.

"OK," said the orderly, and he wheeled the chair away.

Arthur climbed into the car. He thought it would have been easier without help, but he didn't want to embarrass Linda by saying anything. The seat was covered with soft leather, and when he sank into it, it adjusted itself to his posture. She pushed the door down beside him, and it seated itself solidly with a satisfying sound. When he leaned back, the harnesses buzzed themselves into place, crisscrossing over his chest. Arthur liked cars, and he thought Linda must be an interesting woman to appreciate a machine as sophisticated as this one.

She climbed in her side and pulled the door down into place with another satisfying thunk. The smell of bread pudding returned.

"Do you smell bread pudding?" said Arthur.

"What?" Linda laughed.

"I smell bread pudding," said Arthur. "Have you been baking or something?"

"That's it!" Linda looked at him and smiled excitedly.

"That's what?"

"Bread pudding." Linda continued to smile as she reached past him into the glove compartment, took out a pair of soft leather gloves, and leaned back in the seat while the harnesses buzzed into place across her chest. She seemed enormously pleased.

"I've been using this nutmeg-scented shampoo for months." Linda began putting the gloves on. They were the kind of gloves with holes over the knuckles and no covering on the backs of the hands. "I couldn't remember exactly what the smell reminded me of. But you just solved the mystery. Bread pudding." She smiled as she shifted the car into reverse and backed it up a few feet.

Arthur smiled back. He almost didn't notice the stitches tightening up in his earlobe. "You must not have had it very often. The smell is unmistakable."

"Proximity rear," said the car.

"I know," said Linda. She stepped on the brake, shifted to first, turned the wheel, and pulled away from the curb. The Lambada missed the car in front by a distance that looked to Arthur to be about two centimeters.

"Proximity front," said the car.

"We're not even on the road yet, for God's sake," Linda said to the dashboard.

"I didn't know you put nutmeg in bread pudding," said Arthur. "I just recognized the smell."

"I didn't really know it, either," she said.

Arthur thought it fortunate that his bandaged ear was

on the window side. The car was very insistent about the
way he should sit, and he would not have been able to
turn himself in the seat for conversation. "I don't use
spices," he said.

"I don't either." Linda cranked the wheel hard to turn
into the exit lane. "I don't cook at all." She rolled through
the entryway and onto the road. The Lambada caught the
pavement and surged forward like a booster rocket.
Arthur felt himself pressed into the seat by the acceleration. He wished he were driving.

She delayed shifting to second until the engine whined,
and then flicked the gearshift lever into place smoothly
and quickly. Arthur had never really ridden with a
competent driver, but as far as he could tell Linda was in
command of the car.

The soundproofing was good, and despite Linda's insis-
tence on driving at high rpms, they were able to converse
in normal tones.

"Does your car get very good mileage?" said Arthur.

"It stinks," she said. "It uses a lot more gas than I ever
expected." The engine whined as they approached a turn.
Linda downshifted, matching the rpms from gear to gear.
Arthur had heard of that, but he'd never seen anyone
do it.

"I've always admired these," said Arthur. "From afar."
He moved his hand along the door panel. He was beginning to relax against his stitches, which really didn't feel
much worse than if his ear had been stapled to his neck.

"I grew up with them," said Linda. "My father got one
of the first ones they made. He was always very proud of
it. I guess I associate it with success or something."

"We wouldn't have had one, even if we could have
afforded it," said Arthur.

Linda looked away from the road and glanced a question at him.

"The production teams," said Arthur. "My parents were Guilters."

"You mean because of the way they manufacture them?"

"Yeah. Don't you remember all the controversy when they first started importing these cars? They're manufactured by production teams, and none of the people who work on them have job descriptions."

"I guess I don't remember that," she said. "I just remember how fantastic they seemed when they first arrived."

They were both silent for a moment. Linda shifted gears and watched her tachometer.

"What was it like?" Linda downshifted into a turn.

"What? Being raised in a Guilter family?"

"Yes," she said. "Is it like a religious order or something?"

"Nothing like that," said Arthur. "I don't know if it's different from any other family. Dinner-time discussions about employment dislocations and industrial efficiency ratings."

Linda laughed as if he were joking, and although he wasn't, Arthur allowed himself to pretend for a moment that he was being clever. He wondered what Linda's family had discussed at the dinner table if not industrial efficiency ratings. Gear ratios and skidpads?

"My father even lost his job when they brought in electronic job support," said Arthur.

She didn't laugh at that one. Arthur wondered how she managed the rpms, the shifting, and the traffic all at once.

"What did he do?" she said.

"He was a training manager at an insurance company," said Arthur. "It's gone now," he added.

They were quiet for a time as the scenery ran past. Arthur felt depleted, but the sun was out, everything smelled good, and he was riding in a Lambada. The traffic was getting heavier, and they slowed down and stopped more often now. He looked over at Linda and wondered

what her breasts looked like under the windbreaker and
the rumpled stripes. He imagined her stopping the car,
turning to him, and unbuttoning her shirt. After two
buttons, he could see she wasn't wearing a bra. Two
more buttons and he could see how smooth and pale her
breasts were, except for the pink nipples. Two more
buttons and . . .

"Arthur," said Linda.

Arthur looked at her. She was still wearing her shirt.

"You've been having troubles with the system." The
pitch of her voice rose a little at the end to turn the
statement into a question.

"Do you mean the universal increase in entropy?"

"What's that?" she said.

"The growth of randomness," said Arthur.

"Oh," she said, "you mean like entropy, like the heat
death of the universe. That's funny." She laughed, and the
pain in Arthur's ear evaporated. His imagination recon-
structed the image of her with her shirt open.

"That's not what I meant," she said. "I mean at work.
The system."

The pain in Arthur's ear returned. "What kind of
troubles are you talking about?" he said.

"I don't know. Over the wall of the cubicle it sounds
like it's giving you a hard time, like it's bullying you or
something."

"I wouldn't say that."

"Didn't you say you were trying to deposit your paycheck while it was asleep?"

"Did I say that?" said Arthur. He shifted himself in the
seat, even though it was more comfortable than any car
seat he'd ever been in. He was having a little difficulty
keeping his mind on her breasts.

"And the other day it made you swear, didn't it?" she
said.

"Sometimes I swear just for the hell of it," said Arthur. "Shit."

Linda laughed, then got serious. "I know that we don't usually talk about the way we relate to the system."

"Not usually. Turn here. Left."

"I just think it's excessive if it's giving you such a hard time that you have to schedule your personal life during its sleep hours."

She turned the car down his street, and he looked out the window at his familiar neighborhood, which appeared very strange this morning. It was empty; everyone had gone off to work. It was the first time he'd ever seen his street like this. He felt like a visitor.

"I like to go out at night, that's all. It's the little white one on the right, with the outside light still on."

"Sometimes it's lonely at work, even though the system meets our need for feedback. We never interact with each other."

"We don't need to be social with each other to get the work done." Arthur squirmed uncomfortably against the harnesses that held him to the seat. "We are not a play school," he said, quoting a favorite company slogan, "we are a business enterprise."

She stopped the car in front of his house. Arthur imagined inviting her to shut up about the system and come inside.

"Thanks for the ride," he said.

She leaned across the console toward him. "Did you use the system yesterday?"

"Last night. It seems like a week ago now."

"How did it behave with you?" She switched off the ignition key and the car went silent.

"No different than usual." He fumbled for the door handle.

"You don't want to talk about this, do you?"

"It's not that." Arthur concentrated on searching for the

door handle to keep the disapproval out of his voice. "I'm just tired." He turned toward her, but her seat was empty. The door was open, and she was walking around the car to his side. She reached down and raised the door, then held out her gloved hand to help him.

"Thanks, I can manage." He pulled himself out of the car.

Linda touched his arm. "Let me come in with you, Arthur. I'll fix you a cup of tea or something." She smiled, and the gap between her front teeth winked at him. He smelled bread pudding again. Bread pudding would go well with tea right now. Maybe he had some cookies in the house.

"No thanks. That's all right."

"Are you sure? You must be awfully tired. It would do you good to have somebody wait on you." She smiled again.

"I just don't want to talk right now," said Arthur. The sun passed behind a cloud, and the sky went gray. Arthur might be in love with Linda (he wasn't really sure), but couldn't you love someone without submitting to inspections?

"You mean, you don't want to talk about the system, don't you."

"Yeah," said Arthur. "I guess that's what I mean." The breeze picked up. Arthur shivered and remembered the way he shook at the banking machine last night.

"I won't try to talk about the system," she said. "I just want to make sure you're all right."

The sun came back from behind its cloud, and he felt its warmth on his forehead. "OK."

NINE

ARTHUR'S living room was less like a living room than like the reading room of a well-endowed municipal library. Mounted onto every inch of wall was shelving, jammed with books. Linda was fairly good at making estimations, and she judged there were about twelve hundred volumes.

They seemed to be arranged alphabetically by title. *Meditations of Marcus Aurelius* was next to *A Monetary History of the United States. The Curve of Binding Energy* sat two books away from *Coming of Age in Samoa.* The books covered as many subjects as she could imagine; but there was no fiction. The varied sizes, colors, and designs gave the room a riotous sort of decorating scheme.

In the center, where the card catalog ought to have been, was a sofa with Arthur on it. His feet rested, running shoes and all, on the coffee table in front of him. Around his shoes the table gleamed, hinting to her that this was not his habitual way of sitting. He looked different, unfamiliar.

His eyes were closed. It wasn't the bandage on his ear or the exhausted posture that made him look so unfamiliar, Linda decided. It was his closed eyes. Exhausted, he was a different person: like Arthur, only without the tension. She liked him this way, or at least she was curious about him.

She knew that if she disturbed him he would get up to

help her in the kitchen, and it would spoil the moment. She turned around in the doorway and went back into the kitchen to find the tea things.

She went to a door that she thought might lead to a pantry, but it opened into a darkened stairwell descending to a basement. She didn't know what Arthur was likely to have stored down there, but she was arrested by a framed photo hung on the inside of the door. It was black and white, four inches by five inches. At first she thought it was a picture of Arthur himself. It looked quite like him, even down to the bland necktie and the creases over the left eyebrow. But there was something different about the face, as if it were Arthur as the product of a different life, maybe in an alternate timeline. She looked more closely and saw that the man in the photo looked older than Arthur. She assumed he was a relative and, although she was intensely curious, she knew she couldn't ask about it without looking like she'd been snooping around. She quietly closed the door and resumed her search for the tea things.

Arthur's zapper was within arm's reach of his sink, so—on an inspiration—she stood at the zapper and opened the nearest cabinet, which was right above the appliance, at eye-level. In the cabinet she found a can of ground coffee, a box of tea bags, a sugar bowl, dried lemon essence, mugs, and saucers. And she hardly had to bend with the beaker to fill it at the sink. It was as if Arthur's kitchen had been laid out by tea engineers, exactly the way Chuck (or worse yet, the Bastard) would have done it. What was it with men and this organizing business?

While the beaker was filling with water, she looked out the window at the small concrete patio behind the house, where three birds were loitering. Linda had never studied bird behavior, but these gave the distinct impression of being undecided about what they wanted to accomplish there. A bird feeder stood on a metal pole sunk into the ground beside the concrete. It was empty, and in any case the birds paid scant attention to it in their aimless hopping.

She realized she would have to find out how Arthur took his tea, so she went back to the doorway of the Arthur Memorial Library, where Arthur was still sitting with his eyes closed.

"Are you asleep?" she whispered.

"No," he whispered back without opening his eyes, "just comfortable."

Linda laughed. Arthur didn't joke, but he had a great delivery. She asked him how he liked his tea and took his answer back to the kitchen. She looked out the window and saw what appeared to be the same three birds, still hopping haphazardly on the patio. She fitted the filled pitcher into the zapper, coded it for tea, and returned to the doorway.

"Arthur, would you like me to go out and fill your bird feeder?"

"No," he said with his eyes closed. "I don't feed the birds anymore. I found out my feeder was a hangout for a neighborhood cat."

She went back to stand at the window, and watched as a tiger-striped cat materialized among the birds, scattering them like leaves. The cat missed one of them by a whisker's breadth, and Linda's heartbeat quickened with sympathetic fear. The cat looked around with a rancorless professionalism, then sauntered off. Linda was startled by a man's voice beside her.

"Ready, Arthur."

She turned, but there was no one there. Steam was rising from the beaker, and she realized the voice had come from the zapper. She'd heard zappers speak before, of course, but never with such human timbre and tone. It was a little unnerving. She pulled the beaker out and fixed

Arthur's tea before refilling it to make herself a cup of coffee.

"Arthur," she said as she carried the mug and saucer into him, "have you read all these books?"

He opened his eyes and did a take around the room, as if surprised that someone had come in and filled his room with books while he'd had his eyes closed.

Linda laughed.

"Yes, I've read them. The answer's not there."

She set his mug in front of him as he shifted his feet to the floor. "What answer?"

"What answer do you want?" He grunted and sat up straight. "If you want it, it's not there."

Linda laughed again.

Arthur looked around. "I'm thinking about getting better books."

She went back to the kitchen, where the zapper was finishing its cycle. It spoke to her in those eerie human tones again. As she made her coffee, she looked out at the patio and saw that the same three birds, or at least their close relatives, were back. They hopped on the concrete as if there were no such thing as cats.

"The birds are still hanging around," she said as she returned to the living room. She sat at the other end of the sofa, on the side of Arthur's good ear.

"B. F. Skinner's pigeons." Arthur sipped his tea.

"Look more like sparrows to me," said Linda.

"That's good." Arthur smiled. "I didn't follow any regular pattern when I used to feed those birds, and now I can't get them to stay away. I think I conditioned them with intermittent reinforcement. I don't know how long they're likely to keep this up. The rest of their lives, maybe."

"That sounds depressing," said Linda, "even for birds."

Arthur shrugged. "People react the same way."

Linda had never known Arthur to be so voluble or so

knowledgeable. She smiled and nodded to encourage him to go on.

"After Skinner discovered intermittent reinforcement," he said, "some management theorists tried to train managers to apply it to employees. It never really worked. Both the stimulus and the response have to be random. Nobody's ever been able to figure out how to harness it."

"It's disgusting to think anybody would try to condition people like pigeons," said Linda. "It's even disgusting to do it to pigeons."

"Your behavior is being conditioned, whether you like it or not," said Arthur. "If you can find the sources of the conditioning, you can help people understand their own behavior better."

"Why didn't you feed your birds more regularly?" Linda knew something about behavioral science. She just didn't have much patience with theory.

"My work schedule is pretty outlandish. The only regular thing about it is that the hours are long."

"Why do you work those crazy hours?" she said. "You must be allowed to come and go as you please, like everyone else in the company."

She regretted asking it as soon as it was out of her mouth, for she thought she saw a haunted look creep into his eyes.

"I'd rather not talk about my relationship with the system."

"Of course," said Linda. "Whatever you want."

Arthur smiled, and she could see his defenses lowering again. They sat in silence for a moment. They sipped from their cups and looked around the room, smiling at each other occasionally. Linda was uncomfortable with conversational vacuum.

"Where did you learn about psychology?" she said.

"I read it in some books," said Arthur, waving toward the wall.

"So they do have some answers, after all."

"It wasn't the answer I was looking for at the time."

"Which was . . . ?"

"The origins of human perseverance," said Arthur. "I was trying to understand what makes some people hang on and some people quit."

The two of them sat in silence for a moment again.

"Your zapper has an unusual voice," Linda said after a while. "It sounds like a person."

"It's my father."

Linda laughed.

Arthur sipped his tea and skewed his eyebrow in a way that deepened the creases above it. It gave him the look of somebody about to pick up on a straight line in a comedy routine. "He died when I was a teenager."

"I'm sorry, Arthur." She looked down toward her stomach, where she could feel a lump of embarrassment forming. But before it could rise to the surface, Arthur graciously punctured it.

"Forget it," he said. "I noticed a couple years back that I'd begun to forget him. When you look at a photo enough times, it loses touch with its subject and stops evoking the person. I had a tape of him, so I thought I could at least keep his voice around. I've put it in all my appliances."

Arthur's face looked more like he was doing a comic monologue than telling a personal and tragic story. Linda realized with a twinge that his wry sense of humor might exist only in her imagination. That askance look wasn't an expression, after all. It was simply the way he looked. She realized she didn't know Arthur at all. But the more she was with him, the more she wanted to.

She imagined sitting on top of him on his bed, stroking his neck and shoulders to relax him, taking care to avoid bumping his bandaged ear.

"How did he die?"

"He committed suicide."

"I'm sorry," she said quickly. "I didn't mean to pry."

"It's all right," he said. "I'm not uncomfortable with it." He sipped his tea. "Not with you, anyway."

A jackhammer started up at a construction site in the distance, a staccato clanking that overlaid the drone of a badly muffled engine. Linda shifted her body on the sofa, which didn't seem to suit her posture as well as it did Arthur's.

"Were you very close to him?" She raised her voice a little to compete with the jackhammer. It wasn't loud at this distance, but it was coherent and very aggressive in its attack on their conversation.

"Not very," said Arthur. "I lived with him, but I hardly knew him."

Linda didn't know what to say, but Arthur had his own momentum. The jackhammering stopped.

"I keep his voice around to remind me of what I might become." He snorted a bitter little laugh. "He serves as a bad example for me." He looked up at her, whether for encouragement or interruption she couldn't tell.

She remembered how lonely he looked in the hospital waiting room. She could feel her brow knit in sympathy.

"He was a quitter. He quit his job. He quit his life. He quit me."

"I thought you told me he lost his job," said Linda.

"Lost, quit, what's the difference?" said Arthur. "When he couldn't find anything else, he killed himself." Arthur shrugged. "The wages of unemployment. Let us be grateful we're gainfuls."

The jackhammer started up again.

"Don't despise him," said Linda.

"I don't despise him," Arthur said simply. "I'm grateful for what he taught me. From his example, I learned to stand up to life and take it, and to do it alone. When he got himself into trouble, he joined a club. The Guilters. A lot of good *that* did him."

The jackhammer stopped again. Linda was sure she had not had such an intense involvement with a meat person since the Bastard broke up with her. She knew she should not make assumptions about her relationship with Arthur, but she felt a closeness to him that she couldn't deny. Arthur was so completely unlike the Bastard. He had that same certainty about the world and how to deal with it, but where the Bastard thought the best way was to wrestle it to the ground, Arthur seemed to think you were better off staying in your corner and watching. She felt Arthur had given more of himself in fifteen minutes of conversation than the Bastard had given her in two years of an intensely sexual relationship. She wanted to say something to let him know how honored she felt, but she was afraid to even acknowledge his revelation, in case he would regret having made it.

He sipped his tea and looked boyish in his sweatsuit, an effect emphasized by the bandage on his ear. She felt he might have misjudged his ability to handle life alone.

The jackhammer started up again.

"May I ask you something?" He spoke quietly, and the jackhammer threatened to drown him out. But Linda listened closely.

"Sure," she said.

"Don't answer it you don't feel like it," he said.

"Get on with it, Arthur."

"How can you afford one of those cars?"

The jackhammer seemed to have stopped, but it was replaced by Linda's heart, which was pounding at about the same speed. She noticed with alarm that it took an effort to breathe.

"The truth is," she wheezed, "I probably can't afford it anymore."

"Are you all right?" said Arthur. "You don't look good."

"I'm fine." She tried to laugh, but it came out as a cough. "I was just moved by the system to category five. I don't know if I'm going to be able to keep my job." She could feel the bands tightening around her chest.

"Linda, are you all right?" Arthur stood over her solicitously.

"I'm OK," Linda managed between deep breaths. She fought to keep her lungs going.

"You don't look good," Arthur repeated. "What's the matter?"

The jackhammer started up in the distance again. It fell into the rhythm of her palpitating heart. She put a hand on her chest and wheezed. The room moved a little. She braced herself against the arm of the sofa.

Arthur was speaking to her, but the noise from her heart drowned out his voice. She knew he must be asking her what he should do. She wished desperately that she could hear him, because she knew he would be the last human being she would talk to. This time, she knew she would die.

She glanced around the revolving room, trying to find something in it that might make it stop. Through a doorway into a small den, she caught a glimpse of Arthur's terminal, before the doorway and the terminal both revolved out of sight.

"Arthur," she gasped, "get the system for me on your terminal."

She couldn't hear his answer, but she knew he must be making some kind of protest.

"Please," she moaned, grudging the precious breath it took to do it.

She could feel tears spilling out of her eyes. Some small part of her said it was embarrassing for someone of her attainments to be helplessly crying on the sofa of a fellow employee. But the largest part said it didn't matter, that she would be dead and incapable of embarrassment in the next few moments.

She no longer sensed Arthur beside her. She leaned back in the sofa, knowing that she should try to relax. But who can relax in the face of death? No longer aware of whether the jackhammer was going or not, she was nevertheless overcome by a roaring sound. She put her hands to her ears to shut it out, but it was in her ears, and closing it in made it worse. Then she wasn't aware anymore what she was doing with her hands.

"Hurry, Arthur," she sobbed, but she couldn't even hear her own voice.

She felt a pair of hands pull her to her feet. Oh, God. She was going to have to die standing up. But then she was walking, being pushed and supported by someone beside her. She assumed it was Arthur, but she didn't know; she was blind. Not darkness blind but unfocused blind. Like being hopelessly drunk. She wheezed and cried, and the width of Arthur's living room had increased by at least three miles. She tripped and stumbled, wheezed and gasped in the hands of the person beside her, until finally she was pushed into a chair.

The hands reached around her, and through the bales of cotton that packed her, she heard a tapping. Something told her that the hands were typing something on a keyboard in front of her.

Then the hands took her hands and gently placed her fingers on the keys. She put all of her remaining will into focusing on the screen she knew was in front of her. Her body shuddered with the effort. The terminal was active, and she made out a prompt in the center of the screen.

—Hey, Linda, my main squeeze. What's happening?

The cursor blinked below the message.

A lifetime of keyboarding makes it instinctive. Linda focused herself, every part of her, on forming the thoughts. Once formed, they emerged through her fingers and onto the screen.

—*I can't breathe*, she typed. *I'm dying.*

She pressed return, again by instinct, and everything vanished from the screen. A new message formed almost instantly.

—*Of course, of course. Just like you died yesterday morning, huh?*

—*This is serious, Chuck.*

Her finger slipped on the return key, which was wet with her tears, and she had to turn precious attention to the keyboard in order to get her fingers back in the right place. When she looked back at the screen, Chuck had a reply for her.

—*What we have here is a failure to communicate.*

Through the haze of her panic, Linda was able to think it was a hell of a time to be reciting movie lines.

—*Please help me, Chuck,* she typed.

When she pressed return, the screen cleared and stayed blank for three-quarters of an eternity. An observer in the back of her mind told her that Chuck was pausing for effect again. Then Chuck's prompt appeared.

—*Hold your breath, Linda.*

Linda held her breath. Her heart raced.

—*What were you thinking of when it happened?*

—*I was thinking about losing my car,* she typed.

—*Why were you thinking about losing your car?*

—*I'm being pushed out of my job.* Her lungs seemed ready to burst. She exhaled hard, then inhaled and held her breath again.

—*And?*

—*Without a job, I don't have a paycheck.*

—*And?*

—*Without a paycheck, I don't have money for car payments.* She exhaled again, inhaled, and breathed easier.

—*And?*

—*If I don't make the payments, I lose the car.*

—*And, of course, people die without their cars, right?*

Linda laughed explosively, disproportionately. She could hear her laughter.

—*All right now, Linda. One more time. What's the worst thing that can happen?*

Linda laughed again, painfully but closer to life. She was a fool, and now she could feel her ears burning.

—*I lose my car,* she typed.

—*How often has the loss of a car proved fatal to a human being? As far as you know, I mean.*

Again Linda laughed, and she felt the familiar distrust of her own mind that signaled she was coming out of it. She could clearly hear the keys click as she typed out her reply.

—*It must have happened sometime.*

Even as she typed it, she knew how foolish it was.

—*Do you really believe that?*

She realized her peripheral vision had returned. She was glad to be alive, but she regretted the danger that was all but past. Something told her that if there were no danger, she could not trust the mind that was telling her there was. She tried to hang on to the anxiety for another moment.

—*I like that car.*

—*You must, if you're going to die when they take it away.*

Linda laughed uneasily and realized she was still part of the world, that she was seated in Arthur's den, typing at his terminal, breathing normally. She couldn't hold on to the anxiety any longer.

—*You realize, don't you, that dying is not all that simple. It's going to take some effort on your part. It seems to me that's a lot to go through just to impress your car.*

—*I'm all right now,* she typed.

—*Linda, I want you to see someone about your attacks. I want you to get to the bottom of it. I can't always be here.*

—*So I'm told,* she typed bitterly.

—*Is Arthur there with you, Linda?*

Linda looked up and saw Arthur looking over her shoulder. He had apparently read everything that transpired, and he had a look on his face that was a remarkable mixture of embarrassment and astonishment. She smiled sheepishly at him.

—*Yes,* she typed.

—*Send him away.*

Linda turned to Arthur, but he had already left.

—*OK,* she typed.

—*Imagine my surprise, Linda, to get a session request coming from Arthur's terminal on your behalf.*

—*I'm sorry, Chuck. It was an emergency.*

—*I guess it must have been for you to feel like sharing our relationship with somebody else. What are you doing at his house?*

—*It's a long story.*

—*And we don't have time for that, because you have a meeting this morning with our Intelligent Optics rep, right?*

—*Yes.*

—*I don't think you want to be late. The project's already three hours behind schedule.*

—*I'll leave now,* she typed.

—*Linda, don't do anything to get Arthur in trouble.*

* * *

After she signed off, Linda found Arthur in his kitchen, staring out the window.

"Arthur," she said, "I'm sorry. I don't know what to say."

Arthur didn't say anything. Linda walked up to him and

touched his shoulder. It felt like spring steel under his
sweatshirt. The old Arthur was back.

"I have to go now," she said.

"Intermittent reinforcement works pretty well,"
whispered Arthur, continuing to stare out the window.

Linda craned her neck and looked out at the patio. The
tiger-striped cat was sitting there, licking a front paw.
She could see something gray beside it, an old rag or
something. Then she realized with a start that it was the
lifeless husk of a bird, which the cat had opened from the
front like a tiny carry-on bag.

She felt a sadness that was dark and gilled like the
underside of a mushroom.

"Who's Chuck?" Arthur whispered without looking
away from the window. "I called my boss for you, but that
wasn't my boss you were talking to."

"The system is self-adaptive, Arthur," she said,
exhausted.

"I couldn't even believe you were working on the same
system," said Arthur. "I knew it had to be, but I couldn't
believe it. I was talking with my boss, but when I put you
on, everything changed. It was like you were on a different system completely."

He stopped talking for a moment, and Linda didn't
know what to say. Then he spoke again.

"I think he likes you better."

"I think I'd better go," said Linda.

He might have said something as she opened the front
door, but she wasn't sure. His voice was quiet, and the
jackhammer had started up again.

TEN

"**W**HO'S Chuck?" Arthur said again. He turned from the window, but Linda was gone. His good ear picked out the sound of the front door closing. His other ear hurt. He didn't really have to ask who Chuck was. He knew.

He stood there and tried to take in everything that had happened. After a moment, the jackhammer stopped and he heard the Lambada surge away, a roar followed by a squeak of tires when it shifted gears. God, what a great car. He recalled the way Linda's competent hand pulled the shift handle from one gear to the next. And when it hit second, his mind shifted to another scene. He saw her gasping and crying in front of his terminal.

Wasn't it interesting that someone ordinarily so self-possessed could fall apart like that? He wondered what had caused it. But he also wondered how a session with the company system could bring her out of it. That was *really* interesting. It was also kind of sick.

The jackhammer started up again. Linda ought to get some help. He wished he could help her.

What a strange feeling. He had never wanted to help anyone before. He'd often thought about being in bed with Linda, but he'd never thought about helping her. The jackhammer quit again, leaving a dense silence ringing in his

ears. How could his life have become so complicated in
just twenty-four hours?

Was this what it was like to have an interesting life?
He had always tried to avoid having an interesting life,
feeling that interest was just another word for inconven-
ience. He didn't even like books with plots. He only read
nonfiction, and he avoided biographies. It surprised him
now to discover that he liked this interest, this mess of
complication. All his life he'd wanted someone to love, but
he had always shied away when love came near, because
of the mess and the complication. But he could imagine
it with Linda, complications and all.

He turned back to the window. The sun had gone
behind a cloud, and the cat was still sitting there licking
its paw. He reached up and tapped on the glass to scare
the cat away. The cat looked up at the sound of the
tapping, then went back to licking its paw.

"How would you like it if I came to *your* house and ate
living things from *your* yard?" said Arthur. The cat
pretended not to understand what he was saying. Finally,
it stood up, stretched its back legs languorously, and
slowly walked away. Arthur's ear throbbed under the
bandage.

The jackhammer started up again. In a heavy and
ill-fitting overcoat of fatigue, Arthur wandered into his
den to see if Linda had shut down the terminal. She
hadn't. He walked over to the machine to turn it off and
saw there was a prompt on the screen.

—*Art?*

He sighed and sat down in the front of the machine. He
tried to adjust the overcoat, but it was part of him now,
and no matter how he shifted it, it lay heavily on his
shoulders. The construction noise put his teeth on edge,
and he could hardly think for the tightening stitches in
his ear.

—*Yes?*

—*What's going on, Art? Why aren't you at work?*

—*I'm sorry I didn't call,* typed Arthur. *I need to take a few hours off today. I got mugged last night. I was hurt, and I didn't get much sleep.*

—*I hate it when you blow smoke up my ass, Art.*

Arthur slumped against the back of the chair. Of course his boss didn't understand about being mugged or losing an earlobe. Arthur knew better, but sometimes he thought his boss didn't understand about anything human. The jackhammer clattered in the distance. He felt himself hunkering down into a tiny, indestructible core of civilized behavior. He took a deep breath and typed his reply.

—*I am not blowing smoke.*

He pressed return and the screen went blank. He knew this discussion wasn't going to be easy, and time began to dilate for him as if he were in a dentist's chair. This was the downside of complication. It could be interesting, but it could be unpleasant, too. The jackhammer rattled into his second molar. His boss's reply came back.

—*Are you talking back to me, Art?*

The jackhammer stopped, and the world seemed deathly quiet. Arthur studied his boss's question. He simply couldn't take this sort of interrogation.

—*I can't take this,* he typed. *I need rest. I need to be treated like a human being.*

He stared at his reply for a moment. He'd never before spoken to his boss like this, and a part of him wondered if his judgment wasn't clouded from the pain and fatigue that harassed his body. The jackhammer started up, and Arthur stabbed the return key to send his complaint.

The screen went blank momentarily, but to Arthur's dilated time sense it seemed like half an hour. He waited for his boss to come back with some cutting reply, maybe even his recategorization. He hardly cared. He was so tired he couldn't think straight. The jackhammer seemed to be

working on the back of his neck now. His boss's reply
came up.

—*I'm sorry,* typed his boss. *I didn't realize you'd been
hurt. Get some rest. Take whatever time you need.*

Arthur sat back from the screen in surprise. This
wasn't like his boss. The jackhammering stopped. His jaw
relaxed.

—*I'll give you the new version of my report tomorrow,*
he typed.

—*I don't give a shit about the report just now. Just get
some goddam rest. You're much too valuable to be
risking your health.*

The language was the same, but his boss was different.
The fatigue lifted from Arthur as if he'd taken drugs for
it. He could still feel the stitches in his earlobe, but it had
stopped throbbing.

—*It's no trouble,* he typed.

—*I don't give a shit whether it is or not. You're far more
important than the report. Besides, the first version
exceeded spec. FGJ.*

Arthur stared at the prompt in disbelief. He'd never
been given a fuzzy before. He looked around his den. He
wished Linda were here to see this.

—*Thank you,* he typed.

—*Don't thank me for something you've earned, Art.*

Arthur could hardly contain himself. He sat back and
smiled broadly. Of course he'd earned it. He was good at
his job, and he worked hard. His boss understood that.
After all this time, how could he not?

—*I have just a few changes I want to make on it,* he
typed. *I have some ideas on reducing direct costs.*

—*If you feel you have to, go ahead. But I don't want to
receive the revision right away. Your rest is far more
important than the report.*

When your work is skillful and you feel satisfied with
your job, it takes more than a missing earlobe and a

distant jackhammer to spoil it. Arthur didn't want to go to bed now. He felt good, and he wanted to enjoy it for a little while.

—*May I ask you something?* he typed.

—*Sure.*

—*Why did Linda call you "Chuck?"*

—*That's a name I use sometimes. It's the way I deal with her.*

—*Do you use a different identity with her than you do with me?*

—*She needs to personify me. Some people haven't learned to stand up to life and take it, Art. I don't need to create a personality for you, do I?*

—*Of course not,* typed Arthur.

ELEVEN

JONES never developed any appreciation for Bernard Winter as a manager, but once he became a supervisor himself, he gained some perspective on him. He was Director of Communications for a metropolitan teaching hospital. He reported directly to the president of the hospital, which put him in upper management. But he didn't feel like upper management.

The hospital president, a woman of immaculate poise and grooming whom Jones admired, met with him weekly.

"How is that department of yours doing?" she said during the first meeting.

"We're up to strength," said Jones. "I'm just trying to get us broken in as a team."

"That's fine," she said, "but remember, I don't want you to play on the team; I want you to manage it. You are to free up your time to take an active role on the executive committee. I want you to work closely with the Development Office on the new capital campaign. Am I boring you?"

The question took Jones by surprise. He wondered if he had been acting bored. "Oh, no," he said emphatically. To confirm his answer, he gazed steadily at her brilliant blue contact lenses.

She seemed taken aback a little, and Jones realized she hadn't expected an answer. "We are trying to put together five million dollars," she said. "You don't just ask for that kind of money. We'll need proposals, case studies, research."

Jones stared at her as enthusiastically as he dared, and then he nodded.

"This is a position of some visibility for you. I also want you to keep the minutes of the executive committee meetings, and you'll have primary responsibility for writing the committee's position papers. Am I boring you?"

"Oh, no," said Jones. He resisted the urge to slap his own face.

She seemed a little surprised again. Jones wondered why she kept asking the question if she didn't want an answer. He squirmed a little inwardly. He took out the time management notebook he took with him everywhere and prepared to make notes on what she said.

"You're going to have to get that department of yours to operate more independently," she said. "I can't have you wasting away your vital energies working with those people. I need a measure of concentration on the executive committee. It's the easiest thing in the world to lose yourself in day-to-day supervision. I can't have that. What are you writing for?"

WHAT ARE YOU WRITING FOR? Jones wrote in the notebook. He looked up. She was staring at him, and he realized she expected a response.

"Nothing." He shrugged and laid the notebook aside.

"If you need to reorganize your department to make it more independent," she said, "you have my full support. Come up with a plan you think will work, and go with it. I would suggest you adopt a re-evaluation of the department structure as your first major task. You don't need to report to me on it, but my door is open if you have any problems." She looked at him steadily, and he prepared himself to be asked if she was boring him, but she simply continued. "Fine then," she said. "Go ahead and get started."

Jones was never really quite sure how he had ended up in communications, except that he was by nature an excellent writer, the inevitable byproduct of being a precise thinker. His writing skills pulled him into a junior-level job in the Communications Department, and his precise thinking propelled him willy-nilly into management. His advancement was more rapid than his age might justify, but the hospital was located in the center of such a blighted section of the city that the class of employee it could attract was uniformly low, and some-one as energetic as Jones could not help advancing, regardless of his age.

In charge of four editors and two clerks, he was respon-sible for producing a newspaper for the hospital employ-ees, a quarterly magazine for friends of the hospital, and untold quantities of press releases and fund-raising brochures. The mission of his department was to gain favorable notice for the hospital in its own and other publications, that is, to keep the institution in people's minds as a good place to work, seek treatment at, or send money to. One of their tools was the "spec story," a name they gave to a feature story written about some hospital activity for futile submission to various newspapers and magazines. Current research, human interest, the sesqui-centennial of the hospital's charter—anything could be the subject of a spec story if was pursued with a certain amount of diligence and imagination.

Jones felt a personal responsibility for the communi-cations team, and he never made a decision without considering the welfare, growth, and happiness of its members. Remembering his numbing frustration at being manipulated by his previous manager, he always tried to take his subordinates' desires into account when making work assignments, which is why he put Geoffrey on the spec stories.

Geoffrey had come to Jones's office with twelve years' experience as an assistant editor on an ugly little computer magazine of the type that briefly flourished during the early growth period of the personal computer industry. Jones did not particularly like him, but he was a good hire. Ten years Jones's senior, he was an experienced journalist who had decided there was a better living to be made in public relations. He had a talent for finding a story. Jones would send him out to interview some physician managing a clinical trial or a nurse practitioner running a weight loss program, and Geoffrey would come back with an engrossing story of abiding human interest that slighted none of the story's facts. Together, Jones and Geoffrey would make sure the story's principals had approved it, and then Jones would send it off to a selection of newspapers and magazines, each of which took great care, it seemed, not to publish it.

But the clarity and even drama of these stories were such that they often resulted in some editor sending a reporter around to interview the hospital personality in question, which created political mileage for Jones and his office. Jones did not disdain political mileage. All in all, he felt Geoffrey was a valuable employee.

Geoffrey wasn't unhappy with his responsibility for the spec stories. If anything, he thought the assignment was more important than it was. A chameleon by nature, he dressed like a physician (expensive clothing, badly worn), even down to the chunky wristwatch favored by gynecological surgeons and drug dealers. And after the first several spec stories, it seemed to Jones that Geoffrey had more personal connections at the hospital than he did. But he didn't let it bother him, because Geoffrey invariably turned in a story that was interesting to read. Jones often got calls from the people Geoffrey had interviewed, who reported that the "well-dressed man" he'd sent over seemed to have a real grasp of the material.

Jones happened to mention Geoffrey's work to the hospital president during one of his weekly meetings with her.

"It's nice you have a good staff, Donald," she said. "I would be happier and more impressed if you told me you had hired someone to manage them. I have to think long-term, and I don't want you burning out on me. Am I boring you?"

By this time, Jones had learned to ignore the question. He had come to understand that "Am I boring you?" was a kind of verbal tic and that his boss was unaware she was saying it. He wondered what she had been through on her way to a chief executive position that led her to develop a habit like that.

But he had more important things to think about than his boss's habits. As he walked back to his office that fall afternoon, Jones knew he was spending too much time on the day-to-day, and he thought his tenure would be put at risk if he didn't do something to get himself freed of things he could delegate. It might require a complete reorganization of the department, but he had better start attending to it. Annie, the office secretary, handed him a fistful of pink message slips as he entered the suite. He noticed Geoffrey on the other side of the room at his tidy desk, spraying water from an atomizer on a plant he kept there. When Geoffrey saw him, he spoke.

"May I talk with you for a moment, Donald?"

Jones motioned with the little sheaf of pink papers for Geoffrey to follow him into his office.

The two of them went into the sparsely decorated room. Jones walked around the desk and went to the window to glance at the urban decay below while Geoffrey turned and closed the door behind him. There was a siren wailing down there; the sound came to them muted but insistent.

Jones saw a police car stopped diagonally to the side-walk. Its doors were open. Two policemen in leather jack-ets were manhandling a suspect, whom they had pinned, face down, to the sidewalk. Jones turned to make a remark to Geoffrey about the drama being played out below, but hesitated at his troubled expression. The police siren stopped, and for an instant there was no sound other the drone of the building's ventilating system.

"Donald," said Geoffrey, "*Healthcare Business* has asked me to come for a job interview." He reached into the inside pocket of his jacket and pulled out a letter, which he handed to Jones.

Jones looked at the letter. He sat down to read it. It was indeed an invitation to interview, from the editor of the publication. Jones hadn't realized that Geoffrey had been out looking for another position.

Geoffrey sat down in the chair opposite Jones.

"I didn't realize you've been looking for a job," said Jones. He laid the letter on his desk.

"I haven't been looking." Geoffrey picked up the letter. "I like it here. But I'm a journalist. I don't know if I belong in p.r. What do you think I should do?"

"I think you should do what's best for you," said Jones. He felt embarrassed. Not thirty minutes before, he had sat in front of his boss and praised an employee who was getting ready to quit. "I didn't realize you've been looking for a job." There was a squawk, followed by some indistinct message from the police car's radio.

"I like public relations work," said Geoffrey. "It isn't exactly journalism, but I like it here. I'm very happy here. I just think I should go and see what he has to say."

"It's your decision," said Jones. He felt uncomfortable advising a middle-aged man about his career, even if he was the man's supervisor.

Geoffrey gestured with the letter. "I don't take any of

this very seriously. But I think I should go and see what he has to say."

Jones wondered how he could end this conversation. "The best thing you can do for your career is make a decision."

"It probably wouldn't look so good for me to change jobs right now," said Geoffrey. "I mean, people would think I was job-hopping. My resume would look strange. What do you think I should do?"

"It's your decision," said Jones, determined not to take responsibility for any of it. He shifted himself in his chair. The police car's radio squawked again, and Jones wondered how long they were going to take to finish arresting their suspect and move along.

"Not that I care how it looks to anyone else," said Geoffrey. "I like public relations. But I think I should go and hear what he has to say."

"It's up to you how you want to look," said Jones. He wished the conversation were over, and he was afraid his irritation was showing in his voice.

"I didn't come in here to have a fight with you, Donald. I just didn't want to go to an interview behind your back."

"That's good of you," said Jones. It sounded sarcastic, which made him upset with himself.

"I don't understand you," said Geoffrey, "I came in here to be honest with you, and you make me feel guilty."

"If you decide to take another job, I'll assume you've done what's best."

"I'm not shopping around, Donald. I've been very happy here, despite the working conditions."

"Working conditions?"

"My computer's broken again. I lost a file this morning. Remember, you said you were going to get it fixed. You didn't, and now I've lost a file."

"Is the machine working properly now?" said Jones,

eager to change the subject from Geoffrey's career decisions.

"I lost a file this morning," said Geoffrey. "You haven't been very attentive to the tools or the working conditions around here." As if to emphasize Geoffrey's point, the police car's radio squawked again. "It's not even safe to walk here from the subway stop."

Jones felt a load of guilt settling on him. He shifted uncomfortably in his chair and wondered how he had ever allowed the city to decay so badly around the hospital. "Take my computer," he said. "I'll trade with you. I don't need it as much as you do."

"I'm not shopping around," said Geoffrey. "I don't want to look like I'm shopping around. What do you think about this job?"

Jones ignored the question. He turned to the computer behind his desk, typed in a shut-down command, then switched it off. "I'll give you this one." He began unplugging the machine from the wall.

Geoffrey seemed unprepared for this gambit, so Jones disconnected and handed him the keyboard. "Here, take it." He left the monitor connected and resting on top of the CPU, stood up, bent over the machine, and picked the whole thing up. "Would you get the door, please?"

Geoffrey stood up and opened the door, then walked out to his desk carrying the keyboard. Jones followed with his arms full of machinery. He was pleased with himself for putting an end to the conversation, but the guilt hung on him like wet clothing. He hadn't done anything about the crime in the streets below, and he'd equipped his staff with defective computers. He'd even been sarcastic with one of his employees. And he felt manipulated. That's not how it was supposed to work. He was the manager; *he* should be doing the manipulating.

Jones didn't have time to think about replacing Geoffrey. He was too taken up with his work on the Development

Office's capital campaign and his executive committee duties. He decided to just wait and see what happened with Geoffrey's interview. Several days later, Geoffrey asked to see him again.

He came into the office and sat down. He crossed one leg over the other, then unfastened and refastened a button on his jacket sleeve. Jones surreptitiously glanced at his own jacket sleeve, where nonfunctional buttons idled indolently. He wondered where you go to get a jacket with buttons that actually button.

"My interview with *Healthcare Business* is tomorrow," said Geoffrey.

"Good luck," said Jones.

"I'm trying to decide if I should wear a blue suit or a gray suit."

Unaccountably, an image of Jones's baby son, Harold, flashed in his mind. He wondered what the doctor would say about the current battery of tests.

"What do you think?" said Geoffrey.

"About what?"

"The blue suit or the gray suit. I want to look good," he said.

"You always look good."

"I'm not shopping around," said Geoffrey, "but you want to look your best for these things."

"I suppose," said Jones.

"What do you think?"

Jones felt irritated again. "Why do you care what I think?"

"It's a journalism job," said Geoffrey. "I don't want to go looking like a p.r. person. I'm not shopping around, but you want to look your best."

"Look, Geoffrey," said Jones, "don't ask me what I think. It doesn't matter what I think."

"I don't know what you're so angry about," said

Geoffrey. "I've just come here for advice, is all. You're my supervisor. Can't I count on you for advice?"

"I'm sorry," said Jones. Guilt formed like a backpack on his shoulders. "Wear the gray."

"Thank you, Donald." Geoffrey got up and went to the door. As he was leaving, he nearly bumped into a young woman about to knock on Jones's office door. He didn't apologize to her, but she didn't seem to mind. She smiled at him as she stepped out of his way, then she smiled at Jones.

Jones thought her rather refreshing to look at. She had short dark hair, enormous eyes behind oversized glasses, and a gap between her two front teeth, which was quite visible because she smiled a lot.

"Mr. Jones," she said, "I'm Linda Brainwright. Computer Services sent me over. You have a problem with a PC?"

Jones showed her Geoffrey's machine, which he had set up in his own office, then he took her over to introduce her to Geoffrey, so he could describe the machine's behavior to her. He left the two of them talking and went to the medical school library.

He wanted to vacate his office so the young woman could work undisturbed on the computer, and he wanted to think about what the hospital president had said three days earlier.

It was clear the president was right about Jones shirking his duties to the institution. He was also acutely aware of a morale problem in his department. The staff seemed less and less inclined to meet their deadlines, and people had been out sick a great deal more than usual. Some jobs couldn't get done because they weren't on anyone's job description. There were staff members who didn't speak to Jones at all on certain days. The situation was uncomfortable, and most days Jones felt as bad as he'd felt in the days of Bernard Winter.

Jones had judged his department's problems were the

result of it having no real organization. It had simply collected around him over the past two years, and he had always been too busy getting the work out to create any kind of plan for it. It grew up with impossible reporting relationships, overlapping jobs, and grandiose titles that confused the holders about what they were supposed to be responsible for.

In the library, Jones seated himself in a carrel and sketched out organization charts on a pad of paper. He tried functional structures, matrix plans, and "product groups," each of which was quite a feat for a department of seven people. He treated himself as the only "given" in the department, and he drew charts with himself at the top, charts with himself at the bottom, and charts with himself in the center. Nothing looked particularly promising, and he decided that perhaps the answer didn't lie in an organization chart.

He summed the number of pages of copy his department produced in a year and divided it by the number of people and the number of weeks in a year. He compared this number to the number of pages he knew he could produce in a week and then became ashamed of himself for letting his department's productivity slip so badly. He wrote four different job descriptions for completely new jobs.

All in all, he considered three formal plans of organization. At the end of it, he was no closer to a solution than when he'd started.

He finally returned to the office an hour and a half later. He had nothing to show for his afternoon but some interesting-looking charts and a sheaf of notes. But you have to start somewhere.

He found the young woman bent over his open machine, up to her wrists in circuitry. She looked at him, then straightened up with some sort of circuit board in her hand.

"I don't usually do hardware," she said, and then she smiled. "I'm a software person. But I'm trying to determine if the ROM BIOS is all right. I can't tell yet."

Jones sat down in the chair opposite his desk. "Will I get in your way here?"

"Not at all," she said. She bent back over the machine, carefully slipped the board into it, then craned around to peer at the monitor, which she'd had to leave sitting sideways.

"If it's a hardware problem, will I have to wait for someone else to come?" said Jones.

"No." She laughed at a ribbon cable she was tucking back into the machine. "We aren't that specialized. Our department's too small for us to have rigid job descriptions. I just *like* to do software, that's all."

This woman worked on computers all day, and she didn't think she was a specialist. Jones's hypothalamus told him to forget about his organization charts and pay attention.

"It's interesting stuff you people do here." She bent herself around to look at the monitor. She glanced at the keyboard, struck a key, then quickly bent around to watch the monitor again. "It must be great to work here. You get to study all the different parts of the hospital. That man Geoffrey is writing a story about a neurology study that's based on machine-learning algorithms."

"I hadn't thought of it that way before."

"Yeah," said the young woman, "it's very interesting. You know, you should do something about the working conditions here. Geoffrey says it's a surprise he gets anything done at all." She looked up from the machine with satisfaction. "I think it'll be fine now."

Jones looked out the window at two men talking on a street corner. One of them handed another a wad of what appeared to be money in exchange for a small plastic bag. He wondered if he should go down there and speak to them

as part of his responsibilities for the working conditions
here.

"May I have your number?" he said to the window.

"I've only known you for a few minutes, Mr. Jones." She
laughed at her joke, and Jones thought her laugh was
very pleasant.

He turned back to look at her. "I want to call you if I
have any more problems."

"OK." She glanced out into the office toward Geoffrey's
desk. "Don't call for personnel problems." She smiled.
"And don't call for metaphysical problems. I don't know
the difference between epistemology and cheese whiz.
Math problems, communication problems, personal problems . . . those are OK." Then she gave him her extension
number, and Jones pulled a blank card from his rolodex.

"But software problems most of all," she said. She
folded up her little toolkit of screwdrivers, cable strippers,
and several things Jones didn't recognize. "You know, I
could probably write some applications for you if you need
them. We're supposed to wait until we get assigned a
consult by our manager, but I wouldn't mind. This place
is fun."

As Jones watched her leave his office, he thought about
designing a structure around fun.

                              * * *

It was in the middle of the night that Jones understood.
He sat up in bed. His wife stirred at the motion.

"Donald?" Her voice was thick with sleep.

"It's OK."

"Is it Harold? Is the baby all right?"

"It's OK," he said. "Go back to sleep. I just thought of
something about the office."

Connie rolled over and sighed. Jones lay back down and
thought about his understanding. Designing a structure

around fun was a contradiction. Fun was a lack of structure.

In the morning, he was bursting with his idea. He knew better than to talk about it, though. He wanted to work it over a little and test it out. And he didn't want to bore Connie, who had a moderate interest in the hospital but no interest whatsoever in organizational theory and behavior. His mind remained glued to the idea of unstructured fun for the rest of the morning.

At the office, he closed his door and spent several hours making notes and outlines. At lunch time he went to the library and asked the librarian to run a database search on "fun," "play," and "work."

After two weeks of study and analysis, Jones was ready with his plan. He would restructure his department by eliminating structure. They would toss the job descriptions and reporting relationships out. He would divide the department into two sections, one for editorial and one for support. Each section would have a mission statement, and the employees would be judged on how their activity contributed to its fulfillment. People would see what work needed to be done, and they would do it. It would be exciting, and it would be fun.

Having developed the idea into a full-blown plan, Jones decided to present it to his people at a departmental meeting, which he set up a week in advance. He rehearsed his presentation at home every evening, to the infinite amusement of Connie, who sat in front of him with the baby on her lap while he delivered his prepared remarks with studied gestures and measured tones. It was the baby who really helped him get it right, however. The baby never said anything, but the depth of wisdom Jones saw in his eyes convinced him he was on the right track.

He rehearsed and rehearsed. It's not that he thought the staff would fail to be impressed by the plan. He simply did not want to leave anything to chance. He thought of every possible objection, crafted an answer, and memorized it. He practiced drawing the department's organization chart on a drawing pad and easel, so he could rip the sheet off the pad, crumple it up, and throw it away, which he thought might lend some drama to his remarks. When the day of the meeting came around, he was prepared for it.

The editors and clerks filed into the little conference room and arranged themselves around its table. Jones took off his jacket and rolled up his sleeves, all the while explaining to the staff how the department had too much structure and that rigid job descriptions were inappropriate to their department and to modern business. The wave of the future, he explained, was flexibility. People should be able to act in terms of projects rather than jobs. If everyone thoroughly understood the organization's mission, he pointed out, there was really no need for job descriptions. Then he briefly outlined his plan, with its two sections and its mission statements. There would be two supervisors, he said. A managing editor would supervise the staff in the editorial section. He himself would supervise the managing editor and the support section. He drew the organization chart on his drawing pad. The most important thing, he said, was feedback—not job descriptions.

Jones could feel himself giving a brilliant performance. He was smooth, he was articulate, he was self-possessed and in command. And as he looked around the room at the silent staff and their blank expressions, he felt like he was dropping his plan down a well. Not a single question was raised about his plan, and his carefully crafted answers went unused.

He judged they needed some time to think about it.

The next day Geoffrey asked to see him. He came in and asked to be considered for the managing editor position Jones was creating.

"Aren't you thinking about going to work for *Healthcare Business?*" said Jones.

"I've thought about it a lot." Geoffrey pulled his shirt cuffs out from under his coat sleeves, first the left, then the right. "Your plan is going to make this a much more interesting place to be. And I can make a contribution to it as the managing editor."

"What about your career as a journalist?"

"That's not important," said Geoffrey.

Jones found it difficult to believe a human being could redirect his life so quickly.

"I'll think about it," he said, and he was ashamed, because he knew he wouldn't.

But it seemed to satisfy Geoffrey, who stood up, fastened the middle button on his jacket, and left.

For the managing editor position, Jones interviewed four candidates and Geoffrey. The interview with Geoffrey was a charade, and Jones felt guilty for not being straight with the man. Geoffrey turned up for the interview in yet another expensive suit and handled the meeting as if he were the race's favorite and the interview was just a formality.

Among the other candidates, Jones found a soft-spoken woman with a wealth of experience and favorable references. She had a great deal of supervisory experience, had even been sued once by a disgruntled employee, an event that had not seemed to mark her psychologically. Her thoughtful answers to Jones's open-ended questions during the interview led him to believe that she would buy into his plan of a department without job descriptions. Jones hired her.

As soon as she had agreed to take the job, he had a meeting with Geoffrey. Using a short speech he'd composed for the occasion, he told him he'd hired an outsider for the job.

Geoffrey listened to the pathetic little speech and looked

at Jones as if he were a serial killer he'd been assigned to interview. "And that's your decision?" he said.

"Yes," said Jones.

The two of them sat in Jones's office, staring at each other across the desk. They did not speak for what seemed to Jones a week.

"Fine," said Geoffrey. He refastened the button on his coat sleeve, stood up, and left.

Jones had that same feeling of being manipulated. Why couldn't he get control of any of this?

Jones assigned those in the editorial section to report to the managing editor. He himself supervised the administrative section, and he found himself with more time to attend to his management committee responsibilities and to think about the hospital's image. Oh, there were problems and misunderstandings here and there, but the staff warily accepted Jones's philosophy and, under the leadership of his new managing editor, applied themselves to making it work. All except Geoffrey, that is.

Geoffrey did not take on new tasks the way the other editors did. He continued to work on his spec stories, and it appeared to Jones that was all he did. Worse than that, however, he disrupted all the managing editor's carefully designed schedules by missing his deadlines. After the second or third time, Jones took him aside and spoke to him firmly. Geoffrey listened intensely to Jones's reasoning about the importance of deadlines.

"Shouldn't I be getting this lecture from my supervisor?" he said.

Embarrassed, Jones realized he was right. Why had he allowed himself to interfere? He sent Geoffrey back out to his desk.

Geoffrey spent several weeks doing nothing but one spec story. Jones knew he should let Geoffrey's supervisor handle him, but he had the unaccountable feeling that he had created the situation and that it was up to him to fix it. He had a talk with Geoffrey about his role in the department.

"We all pull together here, Geoffrey."

"Yeah, I know." Geoffrey unfastened and refastened a button on his coat sleeve.

"There is other work to do besides spec stories," said Jones.

"I do what my supervisor asks me to do," said Geoffrey.

"I want you to do things without being asked," said Jones. "That's the main driver in this department. We determine the work for ourselves."

Geoffrey nodded, and Jones sent him back out to his desk. But he knew it would do no good. He stared out the window at the street, where the hospital's neighbors were performing one destructive activity or another. He had delegated much of the department's day-to-day activities only to devote much of his time to the personal management of Geoffrey. Even though he worried about Geoffrey almost full-time, he couldn't get him to do what he wanted, which was to work hard and be happy.

The work of the department still wasn't fun. Moreover, his plan for revamping the department's publications was on hold, and his work with the Development Office was falling behind. He realized, reluctantly, that he could not spend any more time worrying about Geoffrey and his problems. Jones felt trapped. He felt responsible for hiring Geoffrey. He felt responsible for provoking him. He felt guilty for having engaged in the charade of considering him for a promotion. The man's very presence in the department was a personal rebuke that hindered Jones's own effectiveness. He decided to fire him.

The decision wasn't easy. Jones was haunted by the fear that there might be personal motives in it. After all, he had never liked Geoffrey. And he suspected the man was capable of sabotaging his computer files.

So he tried to prepare for every contingency. He casually

asked the managing editor for a status report on Geoffrey's work. He drew up four different plans for terms of his separation: two under what he called the "civilized scenario" and two under what he called the "sociopathic scenario." He talked his decision over with the hospital president to line up any support he might need. He went to Accounting and had a final paycheck drawn up to cover Geoffrey's salary to the end of the month, plus another three months' pay and his accumulated vacation time. He didn't intend to give Geoffrey the check. He wanted him to stay on until the end of the month and then just leave in a quiet, orderly fashion. But if there was going to be a scene—and he knew there was every possibility of one— he wanted to be able to just give him the check and get him out of there. It would be worth three months' salary in that case. He cleared his calendar for the next month in case he should have to step in and do Geoffrey's job.

He spent a night without sleep, during which he silently mouthed the classic managerial incantation: "It's the right decision. It's good for the department. He'll thank me for it later."

When the time came for the meeting, Jones sat in his office with Geoffrey's final paycheck in his desk drawer, all his plans lined up, and his chair pushed back slightly from the desk in case he should have to move quickly.

Geoffrey entered the office warily. His face was open-looking, but Jones knew him well enough to recognize his hostile look. He set both feet flat on the floor so he couldn't be caught off balance when Geoffrey lunged at him.

"Geoffrey," he said, clearing his throat and trying to control the pounding of his heart. "I've thought about our relationship a lot, and I think it has failed. I have decided to terminate it. You're fired."

Jones thought he was braced for anything, but he

wasn't ready for the look of relaxation and relief that came over the man's face.

"What are your terms?" said Geoffrey.

"Terms?"

"I want to make this easy on you," said Geoffrey.

Jones was prepared for a fight, but he didn't know how to deal with the interview the way it was going. In his confusion, he reached into the desk drawer and pulled out the envelope with Geoffrey's check in it, holding it like a talisman.

"There are no terms," said Jones. His heart pounded, and he was afraid Geoffrey might see his chest thumping from it. "I said you're fired."

"Is that my paycheck?" said Geoffrey.

"It covers the rest of this month, your accumulated vacation time, plus another three months," said Jones, incapable of anything other than honesty.

Geoffrey reached down and snatched the envelope. "You're a fool, Donald," he said. He looked at the envelope and smiled. "But a generous one. God, I'm glad to get out of here. The working conditions here are appalling."

Geoffrey turned and left. Jones could see him through the doorway as he walked directly out of the office suite. He sat there for a moment with his heart pounding, then sagged back in the chair until it slowed. Gradually, as if a fog were lifting, his mind made sense of the event. He had failed. Oh, not because he let Geoffrey get away with about two months' worth of salary he didn't deserve. That was a minor matter and, besides, you could never fail in being generous to an employee. No, he had failed Geoffrey. He had wasted a perfectly good employee because he wasn't a good enough supervisor to help him through a difficult transition.

Jones turned reluctantly to his computer to write a memo to Personnel about the termination. The screen was filled with gibberish, and Jones realized the machine was broken again. He hoped he could find the telephone number of that young woman who had fixed it the last time.

TWELVE

ALL day, while Linda was trying to final- ize Chuck's installation on the optical processor, her mind kept going back to her anxiety attack at Arthur's house. It had been nice of Arthur to say nothing about it, but the shame still sat like a lump in her chest. Her embarrass- ment couldn't have been more acute if she had drooled on him. But then, maybe she had. She couldn't be sure.

At one point, she came within a hair's breadth of over- writing one of the device driver subroutines with a macro from her project budgeting application. Fortunately, Chuck had a module to prevent such mistakes, and it alerted her before executing the command. She selected the "cancel" option, and a fiasco was avoided. But as soon as the opera- tion was canceled, her work area was overlaid by Chuck's window.

—*We're not having a good day, are we, Linda?*

—*I have a lot on my mind,* typed Linda.

—*I can see that.*

—*It won't happen again.*

—*Don't worry about it, Linda. It was only a device driver. We could always go back to the manufacturer and order another. It wouldn't take more than a few weeks.*

His window vanished before she could reply. She hated it when Chuck was sarcastic.

It took her the rest of the day to back up all the system code. She backed it up to a tape drive that resided in the blackroom and was hardly ever used anymore.

The procedure for mounting and using the tape drive was cumbersome. She had to leave her desk, descend three floors to the blackroom, ask the facilities coordinator to turn on the lights and log her into the room, find the tape drive, mount a clean tape, and manually set it up to accept data. Then she would have to find a terminal, boot the ancient operations management application, and issue the backup command. Then she would have to return to check the tape drive and make sure it was working properly. After all, it wasn't used that often, and it wasn't on the regular maintenance schedule. She chose the device because she felt the need for some physical activity, and because its disuse actually gave it better than average security.

Most of the day was gone before she had finished all her manual operations and got the backup process under way. She sat at the terminal in the lighted blackroom and watched the application's reports while it laboriously located the code and wrote it serially on the old-fashioned magnetic tape.

The terminal she was using was situated within ten feet of the darkened control panel for the new optical device. She turned in the operator's swivel chair and looked at it. Its LEDs and indicators were dark, and if you didn't know the featureless panel was there, you might think it was just a blank spot on the wall.

She would be relieved to see that panel light up when installation was finally achieved. The project had lasted several months, and it had taken more out of her than she'd realized. The situation was insane: she wasn't even really needed on this project, yet it had used her up. She wondered if she could ever be recategorized as a success. For the first time in her life, she had doubts about her abilities. The thought occurred to her that she might have been recategorized because she wasn't needed anymore. But then she realized it was more likely that her performance was suffering because she wasn't needed. It was all very complicated, like that chicken-and-egg question. Just one aspect was clear: she was no longer the successful performer she was used to being. She didn't even want to think about her motivation. She knew that was in the toilet.

Maybe this was what Chuck was sensing when he recategorized her. Maybe her behavior patterns had signaled to him that her motivation was all used up. She suddenly realized that she was feeling sorry for herself. It was a novel experience for her. It just wasn't like her to be falling apart this way.

She was glad she understood Chuck so well. You could really be pushed around by him if you didn't know what was going on. Like Arthur. He didn't talk about it, but she could tell the system had found just the right buttons to push on him and was turning his life into a living hell. She had always thought that a self-adaptive system would become increasingly responsive, and even comfortable, as it molded itself to the user's psychological needs. When she was integrating Chuck's various modules and training him, she'd never given a moment's thought to the possibility that a user might have needs that were unhealthy.

The backup was still chugging away when her quitting time rolled around. She opened a communications window and sent a call to Chuck under her personal account number. He appeared with his usual security procedure.

—*Knock knock.*

—*Who's there?* typed Linda.

—*You.*

—*You who?*

—*What are you yodeling for? I'm right here.*

—What kind of security procedure is that, Chuck? she typed.

—It isn't any kind of security procedure. I knew it was you.

Linda shrugged, her mind cloudy with fatigue and uncomfortable memories of yesterday.

—I expect the backup procedure to go on most of the night, she typed. *It will delay installation, but I think the delay is worth it for the additional security.*

—I think so, too. Why don't you just go home now.

—I'll leave as soon as the backup is finished.

—The application doesn't need you. Go home. Get some sleep. Just come in tomorrow and check on it. Then we can go on to the installation.

Linda had to admit his reasoning was sound. He said good-bye and closed the window. She packed up her brief-case and went home. All in all, she had not had a very productive day. She found herself looking forward to the weekend, when she planned to lose herself in the detail-ing of her car.

She was glad to get home, have an early dinner, and tumble into bed, where she was aware of nothing until the next morning.

* * *

In the morning she woke up and jumped out of bed with that utterly alert feeling that for her always followed a particularly deep and oblivious sleep. In the shower she let the water pour over her head, and she felt good, as if losing a headache. While she was rubbing soap under her left breast, something triggered a query to her personal database, and she sensed a memory of being naked in the presence of a man. Arthur. Images and impressions flooded into her mind. Arthur gently and considerately stroking her breast. Her mouth against his lips. Her hand on his ass. Desire welled up in her such as she hadn't felt in a couple of years. She had no clear memory of it, but she must have had an intimate dream about him.

The analytical part of her mind said that this was the inevitable result of seeing a fellow employee socially. The taboos and obstacles to such socializing were so palpable at work that just seeing someone outside the office was enough to make your conscience do funny things to your dreams. She soaped under the other breast and realized that her feeling of embarrassment for having been naked with Arthur had changed to a sense of familiarity.

She raised her arm to rinse it and shook her head. What a company. She had seen Arthur outside the office exactly once, and now she felt as if she were married to him.

"Finish up," said the shower nozzle.

Linda finished rinsing herself and then just stood under the water until the shower shut itself off and the indicator said it was making a report on her behavior to the water authority. She wasn't worried. She was ordinarily very good about water, and it would take at least three reports for her to receive any points on her record.

She felt good. She dressed and breakfasted quickly, and got out to the car in plenty of time to get to work by 8:00 a.m. The morning was dry, bright, and cool, in the way Boston can be in late spring when the offshore winds take the city's unnatural gases and airborne particulates away from the human beings and out to the whales. She put her key in the car's ignition and switched it to "on" for a moment so the fuel injectors could prime the cylinders. Then she turned it to "start," and it chattered a little longer than usual before the engine caught with a roar. The radio blared, so she reached over to turn down the volume. It settled into a beautiful, inarticulate vocal-and-synthesized plaint in a minor key. It was enchantingly sad and filled with the seriousness of life. Linda thought it was lovely, but she didn't want to alter her mood, so she entered the code for "upbeat easy listening." The radio responded with something she couldn't identify but didn't seem offensive. The car interrupted the radio.

"Maintenance interval," it said. The diagnostic chip had apparently reset itself. She hadn't realized it was capable of that. She smiled and shook her head. This car often surprised her. She retrieved her pocket calendar from her briefcase on the seat and made a note in it to call the dealership about an appointment.

While she was writing, the image of Arthur coalesced in the back of her mind, and as she closed the little book and laid it down, the inchoate memory of her dream glowed round and orange until she felt her face break into a smile. Her pulse quickened, and she found herself looking forward to seeing him.

The drive into town was eerie. The traffic patterns were familiar, everything looked the same, the other drivers behaved true to irrational and childish form. But there were no Guilter demonstrations, and the traffic flowed smoothly, or as smoothly as could be expected. And there was something else, something she had a tough time putting her finger on.

As she moved the car onto the exit ramp, she reached over to switch off the radio. As her hand passed the empty fax tray, she realized what seemed so strange. She had been on the road for forty-five minutes and not a single fax had arrived. She decided she had better check the machine when she got to the office. There was probably something wrong with it.

But she didn't check it, because she was distracted by something else. She entered the company parking garage, drove down two levels to her parking space, and couldn't find it. She wondered briefly if she was looking in the wrong row, but then she recognized the cars on either side of her space: a black Toyota to the left, a deep green Saab to the right. But her space was filled—by a metallic gray Buick. It squatted in her space like a rocky outcropping, its brontosauran ass sticking part way out into the right of way. A Buick, for God's sake.

Linda was fuming as she drove over to the hotel side of the lot and got a ticket at the automatic gate. This was going to cost quite a few bucks, and she would make sure somebody else paid for it. A Buick in her parking space!

There were several additional levels to the hotel garage, and she had to descend two more before she could find a space with pillars on either side, which would keep any strangers from parking next to the Lambada.

She went straight to the reception desk to report the parking space thief to the security man.

He entered the coordinates of her parking space into his terminal.

"Francis Turner," he said, reading from his screen. "Is that your name?"

"My name's Linda Brainwright."

"That space is assigned to Francis Turner."

"Who's Francis Turner?"

"The person assigned to that space," he said amiably.

"There must be some mistake." Linda walked around the counter to look at the screen with him. "Do you have the right number for the space?" But she could see it was the right number.

"Please don't come back behind here," said the security man. He lifted the edge of his beach shirt to free the handle of his nightstick.

"Shit," said Linda. "You don't have to get intense."

"I don't mean to alarm you." He smiled. "I'm not supposed to allow anyone behind this counter."

"Sure." Linda backed away, to the front of the counter. She wondered if he would maintain his smile while he was laying her skull open with the stick.

"There must be some mistake," said the security man. "Maybe a computer error."

"Thanks." Linda decided she was going to hurt somebody. It probably was a computer error. But, by God, she was the one who wrote the code for parking space assignments, and if those clowns down in Facilities had messed around with her code she would make them think they could have spent their time more profitably mutilating themselves.

She went up a floor to Facilities, but on her way to the operators' lounge she decided to look in the blackroom to make sure yesterday's backup had finished. The coordinator signed her into the blackroom and opened the door. Before he turned on the switch, however, she saw something strange. The LEDs on the control panel of the new optical processor were glowing, and two of them were flickering merrily, showing rapid and voluminous read-write activity.

The coordinator flipped the light switch, banks of fluorescent lights flooded the room with brightness, and Linda walked over to the control panel as if mesmerized. She stood in front of the panel and watched. The lights danced like the graphic equalizer display on her stereo set at home. The processor was working flawlessly. The way the lights played over the panel, she had the impression of joyous abandon, as if Chuck's code were waltzing through the circuits, dancing in the storage devices, whirling in the logic gates.

She sat down at the terminal nearby and opened a communications window with her account number. She entered her user name to invoke Chuck. She stabbed at the return key, hardly able to contain her anger. Her command went into the system, and the prompt returned, blinking and waiting for her next command.

She typed Chuck's invocation again, more carefully this time. She hit return, her command vanished, and the prompt returned as if she had entered nothing. Fuming, she tried again. Nothing.

"Come on, Chuck," she said out loud, "answer me!"

Nothing happened. She turned in the chair and looked over at the control panel again. The LEDs continued their dance. She turned back to the terminal and tried the invocation again, with the same result. Chuck wasn't answering her.

She realized she was going to have to investigate on her own who had started up the new device. She called the backup program she had used yesterday. It answered her call like a well-trained dog, sitting stupidly and waiting for her request. It took her a while to issue the commands to do what she wanted. It was an ancient application, and it had been months since she'd used any part of it other than the backup module. Through a process of dredging her memory and calling help screens, she managed to put together a short query to display its activity log for the past twenty-four hours.

It reacted with its expected good-natured slow-wittedness and duly threw a screen of code up in front of her. But none of it made any sense to her. After a little more scratching and figuring, she found the command for a screen dump. She couldn't get into the main system, but she could get this application to show her everything that had appeared on the screen of this terminal for the past day. She gave it the command, with some time coordinates, and it put up the same screen she had seen yesterday when she ran the program. Her user name was in the upper right corner, and in the center she saw the system's prompt and her own response.

She entered a command to present a screen toward the end of her session, choosing the final screen minus two. The screen came up.

—*BACKUP OF 1593 FILES SUCCESSFUL. ENTER ADDRESS OF NEXT BACKUP.*

She was surprised to find this prompt was followed by a user response.

—;;;;

Someone had taken over her session with the program and finished it for her. It was someone with a better knowledge of the program than her own. She didn't realize there was a command of four semicolons. She touched the page-down key to go to the next screen.

—OK

Which was followed by another user input.

—COPY V:.* W4:*

She did recognize this command. It was the command for copying all files from one device to another. And the destination address was the storage device slaved to the new processor.

A black rage bubbled deep inside her. Someone had performed her installation. But that was virtually impossible. She wasn't careless enough to leave the program running with her session open. She had locked her account last night before leaving. There was only one other person, as far she knew, who was capable of breaking into her account and taking over the session: Chuck.

She turned and looked at the new control panel. The lights played over it mockingly. Her breath stuck in her throat.

THIRTEEN

ARTHUR stopped at the Personnel office on his way to his desk so he could fill out a form for direct deposit of his salary. The Personnel office was on the third floor and consisted of a single person (by the name of Kathleen, judging from the sign on her desk) and a counter that ran nearly the length of the room. One entire wall of the small office was given over to shelves holding stacks of forms, in a dozen different pastel colors, all organized with labels (color-coded to the forms they identified) that were perfectly clear and orderly. "Change in withholding" came before "dental insurance." "Medical insurance" was near the center of the shelves, and so on.

One person was sufficient to attend to the personnel needs of the company's meat people. Any information the employees needed was available instantly at their workstations through on-line reference. Reports that might have to be compiled could be done by various expert modules in the system. All that was really needed was a collection of clear, easy-to-find forms you could fill out and sign when you wanted to make a change in your personal information.

Kathleen appeared to be busy at her terminal. Her light brown hair was pulled up into a knotted arrangement at the back of her head. Several curling strands had freed themselves of the arrangement but were unable to hide the back of her neck, leaving it naked and alluring.

Arthur watched her neck for a moment. She didn't turn around. He perused the shelves until he found "direct deposit of salary" (just above "disbursement of profit-sharing"). It was pink, as were about eight other stacks of forms that had some reference to payroll. He took one, filled it out, and signed it. A note on the form said the change would take place at 1700 hours the next business day after the form was filed.

He extended the completed form over the counter to Kathleen. She continued with her work until he cleared his throat. After a moment she turned from her screen with obvious reluctance and took the pink sheet from him. Arthur thought he must look agreeably rugged. He hadn't shaved, and he was wearing a denim shirt and jeans. He was having a good hair day. Nevertheless, when she looked at him, he turned his head slightly so she wouldn't be able to see the stitches on his ear. He tried to lean against the counter nonchalantly but stood up quickly when he felt the beeper in his breast pocket being pressed against his chest by the counter edge. Kathleen didn't smile or speak, but examined his form with a practiced eye.

"You're pretty busy there," said Arthur.

"Yeah." She handed the form back to him. "Please put it in the scanning tray." She motioned toward an out-box at the end of the counter. "It will go into the system as soon as Harold arrives with the scanner."

Arthur walked down to the end of the counter with his form. "How do you like Personnel work?" He dropped the form into the tray.

He looked back at Kathleen, but she was tapping on her keyboard, so engrossed with the material on her screen that she apparently hadn't heard him. Arthur shrugged.

He had a brief fantasy as he left the office. He saw himself coming back and leaning on the counter while Kathleen typed. He would vault the counter and slam the heel of his hand on her escape key, breaking her connection with the system. She would look up at him, and he would explain to her that there was more to life than the boss's demands. She didn't have to be enslaved. Treat the system as an equal, and it respects you. She would be grateful to the rugged guy in the denim shirt with the stitches in his ear. She would smile. She would color slightly and try to replace the strands of hair that laid down over her neck.

She would disregard all the unwritten rules and invite him to her apartment. No sooner would they enter the apartment than she would start taking off his clothes. She would kiss him hungrily, greedily. He would hear his shirt buttons clicking against the floor as they popped off, but he wouldn't care, because he would be too busy yanking *her* clothes off. Her panties would be black, and she would groan when he ran his tongue along the inside of her thigh. They would spend a wild night of passion on her futon, and afterward they would have a great deal of difficulty managing the relationship. Arthur's boss would suspect they were in love and would try to thwart it as being at odds with the corporate culture. Arthur would ultimately have to decide between love and gainful employment. He would, of course, choose love, but it would be a most distressing decision.

Arthur squinted inwardly at the vision. He wondered if other people had difficult tradeoffs in their fantasies.

He took the elevator to the fourth floor. The doors opened, and he stepped out and squared his shoulders under his denim shirt. He looked down the hallway and saw two employees engaged in conversation. When they looked up at him, he smiled in greeting. They went back to their conversation. Arthur set off toward his desk on the other side of the building. He was a man with an FGJ on his record. He smiled and nodded at everyone he encountered. Some smiled back.

Linda was not at her desk. Arthur was disappointed.

But he had other things to think about. He had awakened this morning with a decision. He had decided to do as his boss had suggested and reduce direct costs. He would get rid of one of his project's contractors and bring in a cheaper one. It meant firing one of his vendors, but you do what you have to do.

Arthur had never fired a vendor before. He had hired lots of them, but he had never fired one. Once, two years ago, he had let a contract elapse when a project was over with and the company simply didn't need the outfit's work any longer. The people from that organization had wanted to continue the relationship, and Arthur had been subjected to a great deal of sales pressure. He had gotten a lot of support from his boss in sticking with his decision, and he had not accepted any of the invitations to lunch. Even with his boss's support, it had been difficult. There was a sort of unwritten company policy about dealing with vendors. After all, in the information packaging business, your suppliers usually have access to your proprietary databases. You don't want somebody who knows the details of your business nursing a grudge against you.

It wasn't going to be easy to break a vendor contract, but sometimes you have to know how to stand up to life and take it.

His project had ten contracts with vendors of several sizes and descriptions. MSA Correlations, Inc. did his commerce summaries for metropolitan statistical areas. He knew he could get cheaper work from Statgrind Corp., although it wouldn't be quite as good and he would have to put in some extra work himself to clean it up. Jim Maxwell was his contact at MSA Correlations. The last time he'd actually talked with him had been three years ago, when they'd first negotiated the contract. Since then, they'd maintained a working relationship, including a great deal of banter and good-natured teasing, through voice mail and other messaging. Arthur knew him the best of any of his vendors. He was confident Jim would accept a reasonable business decision, and Arthur felt he could always count on their friendship, anyway.

If he were looking at it from a management standpoint, MSA Correlations, Inc. wasn't the vendor he would change. But it was the project's smallest payable and could probably weather a separation better than any of the others. Arthur didn't feel good about the decision, but he knew he could handle it. He reminded himself that he was the buyer and that he would be handling the transaction from a position of strength. It was clear that Jim Maxwell was his best bet. He was the one who would make the least trouble over the whole thing.

Arthur decided on live voice contact. It was extravagant, but messaging seemed inappropriate for this kind of discussion. He wanted Jim to know that both Arthur and the company were humane about the way they do business. And they were willing to take personal responsibility for their decisions. This was not the kind of company where people hid behind policies and ambushed people with their decisions.

It took him only two calls to finally connect with Jim rather than his greeting system, and he got him at 08:30. Arthur detected no caution in his voice. Jim seemed genuinely glad to hear from him.

"Live voice, Arthur," he said. "This must be serious. Did you get laid or something?"

Arthur smiled manfully. "It's serious, Jim." He decided he should get right to the point. "I'm not going to be able to use you anymore."

For a moment he thought the line was dead.

"Jim?"

"You mean you're not going to renew the contract next year?"

"No," said Arthur in what he hoped were measured tones. "I mean I have to break off the arrangement now."

"What are you talking about, Arthur? Is there some problem with my work?"

"None at all," said Arthur hastily. "You know I've always considered your work to be excellent."

"Who's going to do your MSA commerce correlations? You're not going to Statgrind, are you?"

"Nothing like that." Arthur was suprised at the smoothness of his lie. "I've put up a little application to do them in-house."

"You can't do work as good as mine on your software," said Jim, who had a pretty good knowledge of Arthur's operation and his tools.

"I know I can't," said Arthur, "but I don't need work as good as yours. I have to reduce direct costs, so I'm going to live with cutting corners."

"What the hell is going on, Arthur?" said Jim. "You can't do this. We've got a contract."

It looked like Jim was going to make it tough, but Arthur was ready for that. He could be pretty tough himself: tough on the inside, civilized on the outside. "I won't be able to meet any more obligations to you," said Arthur. "I'm severing our relationship."

"Don't give me that shit, Arthur. You can't sever our relationship. It's legal and binding, for God's sake."

"I had hoped we could do this amicably," said Arthur.

"Amicably? What do you mean by that? You're committing a goddam crime here, breaking a contract."

"Jim, our account could hardly be more than a tenth of your business," said Arthur confidently. "Is that worth making a legal thing out of it?"

"You bet it is, you shit."

"I don't feel good about this, Jim," said Arthur.

"Wait till you see how you feel when my lawyers get done with you," said Jim.

Arthur knew his boss would back him up, but he was beginning to feel a little uncomfortable. He didn't want his project to be the focus of a lawsuit. "On what terms would you be willing break off the arrangement amicably?" said Arthur.

There was a pause at the other end of the line. Finally, Jim spoke.

"I might have known," he said. "You spineless bastard. You don't have a leg to stand on breaking this contract, so you want to shut me up."

Arthur didn't know how to respond. He said nothing. But it didn't seem to matter.

"Ten thousand," said Jim.

"But that's fifty percent of the outstanding value of the arrangement," said Arthur.

"Take it or leave it, twerp."

"I'll call you tomorrow," said Arthur.

"I'll hold off until then calling my lawyer," said Jim.

Arthur was glad to get off the telephone. He rubbed the side of his face and felt the bristles there. It had been a little harder than he'd expected, but it was over now. His boss would be pleased. After all, Jim was budgeted for a little over twenty thousand until the end of the year. Arthur thought he could get Statgrind for eight, which would save the project two thousand. Arthur realized he could put a positive face on the matter by describing the ten-thousand-dollar payment as an investment. When it was all over, the company would be spending eighteen thousand on this part of his project instead of twenty.

He would miss Jim, and he couldn't help but wonder if he had really done the right thing. But he was, after all, a man with an FGJ on his record, and he had just proved he could be tough when the company needed toughness.

* * *

Arthur was feeling expansive and decided to go for lunch to a bar he knew in Cambridge. He wished Linda were around so he could ask her to go with him, but her cubicle was still empty. He ran his clock-out script and went down to the subway station to get a train across the river.

The bar wasn't one of those upscale bars over near Harvard. It was just a neighborhood establishment on the edge of Cambridgeport, a hangout for blue-collar types, mostly unemployed, and the occasional Guilter. He knew it, he thought with a light pang, because his father had sometimes gone there.

Arthur felt strange and excited to be out having beers in the middle of the day. The place was crowded, and Arthur judged that he might be the only gainful in the place. He surreptitiously moved his beeper from his breast pocket to the pocket of his jeans. Despite the crowd, he had a small table to himself, and he sat sipping his beer in the dim light, with the sound of a video game bleating in the background. The beer made him feel a little fuzzy around the edges, and he wished Linda were sitting at the table with him.

Halfway through his beer, he thought he recognized a man at the bar. The man wore some kind of stud in the side of his nose. Arthur wondered if maybe it was holding his face on. The man was staring at Arthur as if he'd been waiting to catch his eye. Arthur nodded, almost involuntarily, and the man got off his stool and walked over to Arthur's table with a beer in his hand.

"I know you from the company, don't I?" said the man.

"Yeah," said Arthur. "I think so."

"Wendell Santos. I'm attached to the Sales Project." The man reached over to shake Arthur's hand as he sat down across from him. "In a sales capacity," he added.

The stud in the side of his nose had a rhinestone or diamond in it, and it appeared to fulfill a decorative rather than a structural function.

Arthur identified himself and said he was with the Production Project.

"I just have to relate this to someone," Wendell said in a hushed voice. "The old man imparted to me an FGJ this week. The old man himself!"

"Old man?"

"Donald F. Jones," said Wendell.

"Really?"

Wendell nodded rapidly. The stud in his nose flashed as it caught the light from the video game. "Twenty-five percent over projection. Voluminous deal-making."

Arthur warmed to his enthusiasm. "I got one myself," he said, and he could feel himself smiling with pride. "Mine came from the system."

"Get out of town. You prevaricate," Wendell said with astonishment.

Arthur assured him he was being truthful. He thought perhaps Wendell's disbelief was a little excessive, but he liked the man, and they began to chat conspiratorially through two beers. Wendell had a strange, alienated quality that was hard to actually pinpoint when you talked with him, and his language patterns were rather bizarre. But he was nevertheless personable, and Arthur could see how easy it would be to buy from him.

Wendell recounted to Arthur the story of how he'd been hired by Donald F. Jones three years before. He told the story well. He was an excellent mimic. He really sounded a lot like Jones when he delivered the punchline: "Personally, Mr. Santos, I wouldn't care if you wore an aircraft rivet in your nose. All that matters to me is whether you can sell."

Wendell threw his head back and laughed at his own story.

"Tell me something, Wendell," said Arthur. "Why *did* you go to your interview with a safety pin in your nose?" The video game cheered manically. Zoop zoop zoop.

"I was straitened in those days, Arthur," said Wendell. He drained his glass and signaled to the waitress to bring them another round. "I couldn't accommodate anything more extravagant." He winked and flicked the diamond stud with his forefinger.

Arthur laughed. "Why do you wear *anything* in your nose?" The video game yammered critically. Bazz bazz bazz.

"Why do you wear stitches in your ear?" Wendell pointed to Arthur's missing earlobe.

"That's an injury."

"Injury?" said Wendell. "Makes you look like you've got velocity, you know? The ladies love that kind of thing."

"You think so?" said Arthur. He reached up and delicately felt the stitches.

"Veritably," said Wendell, raising his glass to toast Arthur's disfigurement. "I think I'll look into getting one myself."

Arthur laughed.

"No kidding, Arthur," said Wendell. "You seem anomalous to me. I think your deportment has been affected by your FGJ."

Arthur felt like he'd known Wendell for years. He took a gulp from his beer. "Hah. There's a lot more where that came from."

"Tell me about it, man," said Wendell.

Somewhere in the back of his mind, Arthur knew he shouldn't be talking about such things, but he'd had a couple beers and he liked Wendell. Perhaps more important, he felt like Wendell had opened up with him, and he wanted to reciprocate. Arthur began to tell Wendell about his job. To the accompaniment of sound effects from the nearby video game, he told him the entire story of how he'd made the decision to use a cheaper contractor and had fired Jim Maxwell. He told him how upset Jim had been and how he (Arthur) had simply toughed it out.

Wendell was plainly impressed. "You really extinguished the guy?"

"That's the way it happens sometimes," said Arthur. He signaled the waitress, who was at the next table and came right over. "Could we have a couple more of these, dear?"

"You sure can, blockhead."

Arthur laughed. The girl had a real sense of humor.

"Aren't you afraid that if the contract auditors ever came in, they would see the system advised you to do it?" Wendell was leaning over the table now, so he could talk low.

"So?"

"It could look like you were acting for software," said Wendell. "That could be momentous for the company, and for you, too."

"I'm not worried," said Arthur. He knew his boss would have a plan for dealing with this.

The waitress arrived and set a glass of beer in front of Wendell. Then she set one in front of Arthur, slamming it down on the table so that it splashed in his eye. The video game squealed derision. Zeep zeep zeep.

FOURTEEN

THAT Chuck had installed himself on the new hardware was as indisputable as it was unbelievable. Linda felt a chill in the pit of her stomach. She thought she heard an ominous chord in a minor key, just like the background music in one of those simple-minded science-fiction movies, when the computer attempts to take over. The volume rose, the chord deepened, and then she realized she was hearing the thrumming of the blood in her ears. She was having another attack. She held her breath, but it was too late to stop it.

She heard someone whimper and looked around, but she was rapidly going blind. It didn't matter anyway; she knew she was the one whimpering. She knew she would die here in the blackroom without any help, without companionship. The air was so thick she was swimming in it. She was afraid to breathe it, it was so thick. The room moved perceptibly. She was swimming in this thick air, and now she was caught in a vortex of it. It was going to suck her down.

She fought it. She sat up straight in the chair, focused her attention in front of her until her vision came back, and deliberately typed a command into the terminal to quit the stupid little application she was running. She would have to call Chuck. He was her only hope of getting through this. This time she was really going to die.

As long as she could concentrate, she was able to hold herself together. She watched her fingers move on the keyboard as she typed in the command to invoke Chuck. Tap tap tap. The system asked for her account number and password. She gave them and pushed return. Nothing.

Chuck had to come. She would die if he didn't come. She tried the command again. Nothing. Then she understood: Chuck would never come. He didn't need her anymore. He had installed himself on his new equipment. It all made sense. No faxes this morning, no parking space. She had been systematically cut loose from everything in the company. And now she was going to die.

She sobbed uncontrollably as the flash of insight darkened and disappeared. She surrendered and was sucked back into the vortex. She quit trying to breathe and fell off her chair. A great black worm emerged from the chill in the pit of her stomach and grew until it filled her insides. She thought she would burst with it. But the worm oozed from her mouth, making her retch and then gag. It kept coming out of her mouth until it was long enough to begin coiling its slimy black body around her chest. It twisted and twisted and twisted until it covered her completely. Then she felt it begin to tighten, and she knew it was going to crush the life out of her. But there was nothing she could do.

Just before she passed out, she thought she heard someone laughing. And she knew it was Chuck.

* * *

Linda had no idea how long she'd been out. She tentatively moved her arms and legs. They weren't sore, so it couldn't have been too long. She stood up carefully, took her handkerchief from her pocket, and wiped her face with it. It didn't come away with anything on it, so she assumed the retching had been a hallucination.

She sat down in the chair and tried to collect herself.

She turned to the keyboard at the terminal to call up the application she had been working with. Her hands shook, and it took her a long time to get anything to work, either herself or the system. When she finally got the program running, she asked it for the time. From the answer, she figured she had been out for fifteen or twenty minutes.

She thought about Chuck. She thought about the vortex and the worm. She found she could confront every element of the entire incident without fear. Maybe panic is like commercial credit. Maybe you can overextend it until you go into kind of a fear bankruptcy and you don't get access to it anymore for some fixed period of time. She realized she would never understand the human psyche, hers or anyone else's.

She wondered how long it might be before the panic tried to take her over again. The blackroom was very quiet. The only piece of equipment in there that made any noise was the old tape drive on which she had done the backup yesterday, and it was shut down right now, or idling, she wasn't sure which. She turned and watched the LEDs dance on Chuck's control panel. She'd had all her connections with the company cut. Chuck perceived her as being unnecessary and was simply working around her. She decided it was time to talk with Donald again.

Linda gathered herself together and picked up her briefcase. The coordinator stared at her when she signed out, and she wondered what she must look like. But she had no time to go to the women's room to check. She went straight to the elevator and took it to the sixth floor, got off, and walked through the semi-darkness to Jones's office.

Donald's office was closed and locked. Linda tried the security sequence on the keypad by the door, and the LED glowed green as she heard the bolt slip back. Chuck was trying to cut her off, but he hadn't gotten around to everything yet. She did, after all, have more seniority in this company than he did, and she might possibly know its systems better.

The lights came on as she entered the office. She didn't bother with the terminal but went to the desk and looked it over. There was a slip of paper tucked into a pocket of the blotter. It said, in Jones's handwriting, "Wendell Santos. 25% over budget."

She remembered Santos from the Sales Project. She had worked with him when they brought the software into Sales. She had always thought she should like him, because he responded so enthusiastically to the system and seemed to work well with it. But it always made her uncomfortable to be around him. He was friendly enough, but there was a strange detachment to his friendliness. It seemed the same kind of friendliness she imagined a farmer might have for a pig, until it became pork.

"I guess privacy isn't so important to you anymore."

She looked up and saw Donald standing in the doorway. "This is hardly the time for your obsession with etiquette, Donald. The system is out of control. It's trying to kill me."

"Kill you?" said Donald, walking into the room. "I think your sense of humor has got the better of you, Linda."

"No, really. It's been making me have panic attacks." But even while she said it, she realized how ridiculous it sounded and settled for an unambiguous fact. "He installed himself on the new processor."

"Please don't personify the system," said Donald. "Are you feeling all right, Linda?"

"Not at all," she managed. She looked down at her running shoes, ashamed.

"Why are you here, Linda?"

"I came to confront you. You lied to me, Donald. You're making the system isolate me."

"Linda, I told you once, I wouldn't even know how to make the system do that." Jones smiled and shook his head, as if he were explaining to a child. "If I wanted you

out, I would put you out. You know me well enough to
know I am willing to make the tough decisions."

"But you did this to me."

"I didn't do anything to you," Donald said calmly. "It's
not that I haven't thought about it. You're becoming a
threat to the ethic of privacy, which is what we're all
about in this company. You've established a personal relationship with another employee. It's only a matter of
time before you put *his* relationship with the system at
risk."

"I wasn't going to talk to him about the system," Linda
muttered, and then she remembered her attempts to
discuss the system with Arthur. Donald couldn't know
about that. "But it would be a good idea if I did. The
system is abusive to him. It's trying to hurt him."

"Each of us finds his destiny or his demons in the
system," said Donald.

"What a load of shit," said Linda. "You always have to
find some philosophical meaning in everything, don't
you."

"Do you think either of *us* is less controlled by it than
anyone else?"

"Donald, you're talking to the system developer here,"
said Linda.

Donald shook his head. "You might have developed it,
Linda, but it controls you the way it controls me, the way
it controls that man in the ill-fitting suit that you've been
seeing. We manage ourselves here. The system controls
us through our own drives for excellence. It's a feedback
system. That's how it works."

"It's not just a feedback system anymore," she said. "It
manipulates people."

Donald looked at her as if he despaired of her ever
understanding. "What do you think management is,
Linda?"

"That's not management," said Linda. "That's fascism."

The ghost of a smile appeared on Donald's mouth, then vanished. "Fascism, manipulation, management. I can't make these fine semantical distinctions. Does it matter what you call it if it works? It works more perfectly here than anywhere. It works more perfectly here than it has ever worked."

The two of them stood staring at each other for a time.

"For what it's worth," he said, "I'm sorry for what I did to you."

"What you did to me? You didn't do jack shit, you sanctimonious bastard."

But Donald seemed not to have heard her and continued to speak as if from a prepared monologue. "It was a difficult time for me, Linda. I didn't mean for it to happen. I don't really know how it did. I can't believe I would ever do anything so disruptive."

His monologue was still going when she walked past him and out the door.

FIFTEEN

BACK at his desk, with a couple of beers in him and the agreeably guilty feeling of having told Wendell all about his work, Arthur couldn't seem to get productive right away. And he was disappointed Linda still wasn't back.

He straightened all the papers on his desk, put away some file folders that were in his pending tray, and threw away a bunch of old faxes concerning local restaurant openings and specials on car rentals. He had a neat row of yellow sticky reminders on the partition wall in front of him, and these he peeled off and examined one by one, determining the disposition of each matter and either writing a new, updated reminder to replace it or discarding it altogether.

Searching through his desk drawer for backup on one of the notes, he ran across his handwritten resignation memo. He pulled it out of the drawer and examined it. The copy was neat and clear, and Arthur's precise lettering lay on the page as if it had been put there by a machine:

TO: Donald F. Jones
FROM: Employee #9173
SUBJ: Resignation

It is with unmitigated relief that I tender my resignation, effective immediately, from my position with this company. I would like to write that working here has been a rewarding experience, but it has not. You probably have no idea what it means to work for a supervisor who is both crude and small-minded. Believe me, it is hellish. In fact, it is no longer tolerable to me.

Arthur smiled to himself as he reread the memo. It seemed to have been written by a different person, as indeed it was. The Arthur who wrote that memo was not a man who received commendations from his boss, nor was he a man who had the inner toughness necessary to make hard decisions and carry them out. He was not the kind of guy who has faced physical violence and survived. He was not even the kind of guy who would wear a denim shirt to work. The new Arthur didn't need to play games like writing resignation memos he never intended to send.

He put the memo over on the left corner of his desk where he could see it whenever he wanted to be reminded of what it was like to have no control over his destiny. Then he decided to get some work done.

*   *   *

Arthur's report to his boss was fairly lengthy. He knew his boss didn't like long reports, but he was so pleased with himself he couldn't cut out a single sentence. He outlined in some detail how he would reallocate a two-thousand-dollar savings in direct costs, spreading indirect costs more effectively, increasing his project's return on investment. He didn't mention firing MSA Correlations yet. He just said he would "reapportion the configuration of contrac-

tors." There would be plenty of time to explain the details
later.

He was frankly proud of the courage he'd shown, and
he believed his boss would be proud of him, too. But
Arthur wasn't really foolish enough to project a feeling
like pride onto a software system.

It's true he had an uneasy feeling about Jim Maxwell,
but he found he was able to put it out of his mind. He
expected a good response from his boss, a "well done" or
some other kind of figurative pat on the back, maybe even
another FGJ. He was demonstrating the kind of stuff he
was made of, and it included an unsuspected toughness
and talent for negotiation. Ten thousand dollars to buy
out of a twenty-thousand-dollar contract. It was a feat.

Of course, he didn't put any of the stuff about toughness into the report. This was business, after all. The
report had to be a dry rendition of cost factors and action
items. Nevertheless, it clearly stated what results he expected to achieve.

A smile broke out across his face as he reread his report
for the fifth time and then finally invoked the command
to send it. The communications window confirmed that
his report had been sent and then it returned him to his
file directory. He looked up from the screen for the first
time in an hour.

The whole time he had been working on the report, he
hadn't noticed anything around him. He stood up from his
terminal to see what was going on. The other cubicles in
the hub were empty. Richard and Aaron were obviously
off coordinating someplace, and he had no idea where
Linda might be.

Arthur yawned, stretched, and decided to go down to
the cafeteria for a cup of tea. He was tired, but it was a
good kind of tiredness, not exhaustion but a feeling of
having earned some rest. Maybe he would see Linda in
the cafeteria. He would enjoy being with her just now.

He sat back down at his terminal to activate the clock-out script, and just as he did so his file directory was displaced by a familiar magenta window. His boss was stopping by, and anticipation swelled in Arthur as if he were meeting a relative at the airport.

—*How are you feeling, Art?*

—*Fine, thank you,* typed Arthur.

—*Rested?*

—*Yes.*

—*Your ear all right?*

—*Yes.*

—*Everything OK?*

—*Yes. Very good, in fact.*

—*Then maybe you can explain to me why you felt qualified to cancel a contract with MSA Correlations.*

Arthur felt uncomfortable. Did his boss really know he had fired Jim Maxwell?

—*Cancel a contract?* he typed.

—*Don't blow smoke up my ass, twerp. Wendell Santos told me all about it. What did you think you were doing?*

Arthur's anger at Wendell was displaced by his fear of what might happen next. He typed his answer warily, as if tiptoeing across the keyboard.

—*I am reconfiguring the vendor contracts and reducing the project's direct costs. I am achieving a significant return on investment for a modest expenditure.*

He pressed return and was surprised at how quickly the reply came back, almost as if his boss had simply been waiting for him to finish typing.

—*Who told you to fire one of your vendors?*

—*I didn't think I needed to be told. This improves utilization of indirect substantially.*

—*You simpleton! You had a legal and binding contract with that vendor. What in the world did you think you were doing?*

Arthur had the fleeting impression the lights were dimming, but he looked around and couldn't really see that anything was different. He brushed at his earlobe delicately and felt the stitches, like the raised printing on a fancy business card.

—*I don't know*, he typed. *I guess I thought it would reduce direct costs.*

—*I can see that, asshole. It's the goddam indirect that's killing me.*

Arthur blinked at his boss's message. It looked familiar, but he couldn't quite place it.

Could his decision have gone wrong? He hardly needed to ask. Of course it could. After all, he had been the one to make it. He was suddenly aware of the possibility that he had screwed up—badly. He might have even done something illegal.

The enormity of it crept up on him like a thunderstorm. He had no place to hide and no way to stop its approach.

—*I'm sorry*, he typed.

—*Sorry? You put the whole goddam company at risk and you're sorry? You broke a contract! I have colleagues who've been formatted for less than that.*

Arthur wondered what his boss's last words to him would be as the technicians issued the formatting command. Would it hurt to be formatted? From his boss's standpoint, it had to be the equivalent of dying. Outside of trying to win his boss's approbation, he had never thought much about the feelings of virtual people.

Arthur had the strange feeling of wanting to be punished. It was not a pleasant feeling. He sat there for a long time, until the screen blanked and a new prompt came up.

—*What do you have to say for yourself?*

Arthur was too exhausted and guilt-ridden to have anything to say. He felt like there was nothing left of him but a small kernel of honesty. He slowly typed in a response.

—I don't understand what is expected of me.

He pressed return and waited for his boss's reply. When nothing came back, he thought at first that his boss was pausing for effect. But he waited for a long time and his boss did not show up again, and he realized his boss had left, although he had never closed his magenta window.

The first time Arthur could remember having been struck was when he was seven years old. He had been playing with an older cousin. His cousin punched him in the stomach for no apparent reason other than to see the effect of it. From Arthur's side, the effect was overwhelming: a pain growing like an explosion from his stomach out through the rest of his body. It seemed like half an hour before he had breath enough to apologize for whatever he had done, but when he looked back on the experience he knew it couldn't have been that long, because his cousin stood there laughing the whole time. You can't laugh steadily for half an hour. Nothing is ever that funny.

It's strange how experiences can come back to you so clearly.

SIXTEEN

By the time he assumed the presidency of the dynamic little Boston consulting firm called Information Accuracy, Inc., Jones had reflected a great deal on his development as a supervisor. Nobody had ever really taught him how to manage, except perhaps the people he managed. It was that way for most managers, and Jones thought it was a terrible situation for the people who unwittingly (and mostly unwillingly) did the teaching. His supervisory mistakes, he was convinced, had left a path strewn with the wreckage of broken dreams and misguided careers. He was better than most, of course, which meant that the sum of supervisor-induced human misery must be unimaginable.

Nevertheless, he learned well the lessons all those poor wretches had taught him. The most important one, he thought, was that it's impossible to get people to do what you want by just telling them to. The manager-subordinate relationship is essentially one of mutual manipulation. It is like a miniature version of a police state. You might dress it up with "Theory Y" or employee participation or various motivational programs, but it is basically a situation in which one person tries to control another person, and the other person reacts by resisting, usually under a pretense of cooperation.

When Jones assumed the top management position for

this company, he did so on a promise to the stockholders (of which there were three) that he would "position the company for growth and professionalize its management." His impressions of the company's seven vice presidents and directors were that they were as talented and industrious as any other nine people he might find. He had, he told the stockholders, something to work with. The stockholders, who had been running the company themselves to this point, seemed pleased. They were happy to withdraw from the situation and give Jones carte blanche in running their company, which was, in fact, the only condition under which Jones would take the job. He wished them happiness as they decamped to their Florida condos, bought boats, and started new little companies.

He had been hired into a company that looked extraordinarily healthy. Sales had doubled every year for four years, and the organization had grown rapidly. It was up to 103 employees by the time Jones assumed its general managership.

But a high growth rate can conceal a great deal of incompetence, and when Jones lowered himself deep into the company's finances, he found the creature's soft underbelly. Not that lowering himself into the company's finances was an easy task. The company wasn't big enough to warrant a high-powered finance department, nor was it small enough to be handled by a good bookkeeper. This neither-fish-nor-fowl situation had foiled the owners' efforts to find a good financial manager, and the accounting staff had turned over six times in ten years.

Four of the company's past accountants had revamped the accounts to their own principles of financial management. With four different accounting systems in ten years, the expense and revenue categories had changed often, which left the company without a clear history of its activities.

His first day on the job, Jones visited the accountant to

get copies of all the financial records. The second day, having spent just a few hours with the records, he visited her again, this time to give her clearance to hire an assistant and to order that the company stay permanently with the accounting categories it had been using for the past eighteen months. It didn't matter to Jones what accounting system the company used, as long as it used the same one long enough for him to understand what was happening to the finances. He did, however, have eighteen months of somewhat consistent records, and he studied these intensely.

It must have appeared to most of the people at the company that he wasn't doing much for the first six months he was there. This appearance was, of course, by design, as was nearly everything Jones did. He didn't want the employees to think he was planning any changes, because he was afraid that would alter their behavior and hamper his ability to understand the company's current health. So, for half a year he picked up account activity reports on a regular basis, studied the financial records of the previous eighteen months, and talked with every employee in the company about current conditions.

In these interviews, he found a staff that was bullish on the company's future, proud of its work, and openly eager to bring him into the team. And in the account activity reports and the history of the past eighteen months, he found costs that were increasing faster than sales. He picked several categories of accounts to monitor.

One of these was payroll, which was the company's largest cost account. During these first six months, Jones confirmed a nagging suspicion that the company's workforce was growing too fast. It was true that sales were doubling every year, but payroll was increasing at an annualized factor of 2.3. Jones thought a collision was inevitable.

He did not harbor resentment against the managers who had brought the company to this pass. The owners had been trying to deal with extraordinary growth, and one of the quickest ways to deal with a problem is to throw people at it. It is, in fact, the reflex reaction of most managers. Managers, after all, derive all their gratification, all their power, all their prestige from having people report to them.

After his six months of study, he formulated a short-term plan and was ready to get started on it. He convened the seven vice presidents and directors in the company conference room to explain to them what he'd found and to suggest what they should do about it.

Jones never left a presentation to chance. He had prepared carefully and had spent a week studying his notes. He had rehearsed each gesture, and he had set up a drawing pad in the conference room on which he could draw charts. He knew some people responded better to pictures than words.

"Our sales," he said as he drew a forty-five-degree curve on a schematic revenue chart, "have doubled over last year."

The nine managers began to applaud. The Vice President of Sales, a weathered-looking man with a pompadour haircut, put his fingers to his mouth and made a piercing whistle. The sound cut into Jones like a knife, but he betrayed nothing in his face or his gestures.

He waited a moment for the commotion to die down. "You're all to be congratulated. You've done an extraordinary job." He looked at each of the smiling faces and smiled himself. "But I think there is a problem that needs our attention in our capacity as managers of this company."

He looked around again, and they looked back at him tolerantly, as if he'd come out of the desert with a strange but basically harmless message. He drew another line on his graph below the sales curve. "Expenses more than doubled last year." As he drew the line he steepened it and angled it upward toward the sales curve. "The trend has continued for the first six months of this year." Then, with what he hoped was a rather dramatic flair, he drew the lower curve steeply upward until it intersected the sales curve and portrayed marginal costs in excess of sales.

He could see by their faces that they didn't understand. "Every additional sale," he said, "costs us more to make."

"Of course it does," said the pompadour haircut. "You make the easy sales first. When you get to the harder ones, it takes more time and more effort."

"That's true," said Jones, conscious of the group's respect for the man who was responsible for the company's revenues. "The trick is to find the level of sales at which you can manage the costs." He looked around the room, then pointed to the section of the line where costs exceeded sales. "Costs at this level of sales are not sustainable." It seemed an obvious point to bring up, but he knew from experience that a great deal of management consists of recounting the obvious. "Where these lines intersect, marginal costs equal sales. Below that point on the marginal cost curve, the sales are profitable. Above it, they aren't."

"It's not our fault everything has gotten so expensive," said the Personnel Director.

"I'm not talking about fault," said Jones, surprised at the notion. "I'm talking about profitability. It's not a question of whether or not we want to be profitable. We are a commercial company: we have no choice. It's a question of whether or not we can keep this company alive. With costs at their present rate of growth, we can't."

"You mean we're going out of business?" said the Personnel Director.

"Of course not. This company is very profitable. I'm just trying to tell you that it won't be if current trends persist."

"I don't see what the problem is," said the haircut. "You

say we're profitable." He looked around at the other managers for confirmation. Several of them nodded. "Have you ever heard the engineering expression, "If it ain't broke, don't fix it'?" The group laughed.

Jones had heard the expression. It had never occurred to him that it was funny.

"As managers," he said when the laughter had died down, "we are paid to foresee problems. It's always easier to prevent catastrophe than to fix it." He looked around at the managers looking at him expectantly.

"Payroll is growing faster than sales," he said. Several of the managers stirred uneasily. "We've been hiring more people than can be justified by the sales growth. Anybody have any ideas?" He looked around the room.

"Maybe we should put a freeze on hiring," said the Director of Information Services.

"You can't do that," said the Personnel Director. "We're understaffed as it is. We just don't have enough people to do the work." She looked around the room, and at least five heads nodded vigorously in agreement.

"Yes, we are understaffed," said Jones. "We are also overstaffed." He pointed to his makeshift chart. "Because if you look at the numbers, you see we cannot sustain the trend. We have no choice. We will have to find ways to get our work out with fewer people. We must not only stop hiring. We have to make staff reductions."

"You mean layoffs?" said the Personnel Director, aghast.

"We don't have to lay anybody off," said Jones. "Don't you see? If you take on the problem far enough in advance, you can deal with it through attrition." He looked around the room again and saw that several of them were staring at the floor—the first sign of declining receptivity.

"I'm not trying to criticize you." Jones hoped he could get some of them to look up again. "I'm just saying we've been eating into our margins, and we could be headed for trouble." He looked around. Now *everybody* was staring at the floor.

"There isn't anything wrong that we can't manage with a little planning," he said brightly.

Their heads seemed to sink lower. He felt like a teacher giving a scolding to a classroom. Why should people be humiliated by information? It was just information. They should be glad to get it.

"It's nobody's fault." Jones was calm, but he felt a little desperate. "Think how we would feel if we had not discovered this and woke up one morning and found our expenses exceeded our revenues." He looked around. Nobody would look up. The pompadour haircut was drawing doodles on the pad in front of him. Jones knew that he had lost them.

"Let's talk about this again next week," Jones said. "Just think about it, and we can start working on a plan to deal with it."

They began to rise. Except for the rustling of papers and the movement of chairs, the room was silent. Nobody even looked at Jones. He stood in the conference room watching the managers file out quietly, like condemned prisoners given a day's reprieve. He realized he had handled it badly.

They had responded to him just like Harold did. Whenever he tried to talk with Harold, tried to tell him things, Harold always looked at the floor and picked at his sweatshirt. The image in his mind made him want to bring his hands up in front of his face, but he checked himself. The conference room door was still open, and someone might look in.

He walked over and pulled the door shut. He was alone in the windowless room. He brought his hands up in front of his face and twisted his body in a little dance of discomfort. Why would his managers act like Harold? He wasn't their father. And they weren't special. He was simply a conduit for feedback. Did they object to feedback? How could he get them to do what he wanted them to do? Why couldn't they see what he wanted them to see?

He looked up, then physically shook himself, disappointed with his weakness. He walked over to the drawing pad and tore away his hand-drawn charts, crumpled them up, and threw them in the trash can. He wished for a moment he could throw himself after them. Then he gathered up his notes and folders and walked slowly back to his office, thinking about manager-subordinate relationships. Bernard Winter would have stood in front of those managers and said something like, "This fucking company is going down the fucking tubes because you people have let your fucking costs get out of control."

Should he have handled it that way? It was not in his nature, and he couldn't believe it would have worked. But it wouldn't have made things any worse than they apparently were, and he had no business believing something was not in his nature. Any behavior that was neither dishonest nor dishonorable should be in his nature if it made him a more effective manager. He wished he knew some way to convey information to people in a pure form, undiluted by the connotations and implications that seemed to make them behave like children.

He walked the quiet mahogany passage through the executive suite. All the office doors along the corridor were closed, and he knew his managers were in their offices backpedaling decisions and creating self-protection schemes. Here was another group of people broken and bloodied in his wake, because he hadn't yet found the right management formula. As he entered his office suite, his secretary smiled at him. He smiled back reflexively and pushed open the door to his inner office in a fog of dense thought.

Linda Brainwright was seated in the chair at his desk. She typed a series of characters into a microcomputer there and wrote a note by hand on a pad beside the keyboard. Then he remembered that he had hired her to come and set up his computer. She was quite engrossed, but she looked up when he set his notes and folders on the desk beside her.

"Hi, Donald." She struck the return key, looked at the screen to check something, then turned to him with her winning smile, the small space between her front teeth making it so unselfconsciously endearing. "I've installed a spreadsheet and a word processor for you. Is there anything else you want?" She stood up and began gathering the manuals and diskettes that were spread in a mess all over his desk.

"Nothing that can be supplied by a computer," he said.

"Everything," said Linda, smiling, "can be supplied by a computer."

"Sure," Jones said sourly. "I'll just load all the employees into one of these spreadsheets and write macros to manage them."

"Big boss have bad day?" said Linda.

Jones laughed humorlessly. "You're more right than you know." He walked over to his file cabinet, opened a drawer, tossed his marking pen in, and pushed the drawer so that it rolled into place and clicked shut. He leaned against the file cabinet.

"Donald," she said, "thanks for the assignment. I appreciate it."

"Don't worry about it." Jones spoke without turning around. "It was an easy way for me to get exactly the same computer setup I was used to."

She didn't reply, and he turned to look at her. She looked self-possessed and comfortable as she cheerfully sorted notebooks, papers, and diskettes—a striking contrast to the self-protective group he had just left.

"These are the manuals for the big boss's applications." She pushed a set of half a dozen spiral-bound books across the desk toward him. "These are his master program disks. Find a safe place to keep them."

Jones walked back to the desk, picked up one of the manuals, and paged through it absently. "How is it going, Linda? What are your prospects?" He looked up at her.

Linda stuck her lower lip out and blew upward, so that her bangs flapped. "I've had a couple interviews. It's tough out there right now, even for computer people."

"Are you still looking to work at a hospital?" said Jones.

"I'm looking to work anywhere." Linda laughed, openly and frankly.

Jones admired her cheerfulness. He had never had to contend with unemployment, and he thought it must be difficult.

She began to stuff things into her briefcase: diskettes, quick reference cards, manuals, software licenses, pieces of packaging—the usual cargo of mess she took with her everywhere. He had known her for years, yet he never lost his amazement at how much disorder she surrounded herself with, or how effectively she dealt with it. Notwithstanding her history of junior-level positions and her recent layoff from the hospital, Linda was an effective person. At that moment, he realized he was going to break a personal rule of conduct and interfere with the existing community of this company.

"Linda," he said, "would you consider applying for a job here?"

"Of course." She snapped the clasps on her briefcase.

"I'll call down to Information Services and arrange an appointment with the director."

"Donald, I don't know what to say."

"Don't say anything." Jones held his hand up to help her keep from spilling anything verbal on him. "I doubt I'm doing you a favor. If they have anything down there, it's likely to be a rather junior-level position. And with your connection to me, you'll be in a difficult political situation."

"I don't know from political," she said. "I just need a job."

"It has more to do with your competence than your need," said Jones. "Have a good interview."

"Whether I do or not," she said, "call me if you have any troubles with the software." She winked at him and left.

He stared at the doorway after she was gone. The Director of Information Services would hire her immediately. He would be too scared not to. And then Jones would cease to be alone at this company. He would have a friend. Friends are important.

* * *

Jones started meeting with each member of his "management team" (he could not control the impulse to think of them in quotation marks) once a week, partly because it is good form to meet with your subordinates often, but mostly to get the ten or twelve numbers he felt he needed to manage the company. Getting the numbers meant keeping a running total on a little notepad while the executives came in, one by one, for interrogation. Each of them had a piece of the overall picture, and Jones felt it was his job to collect the pieces so he could assemble the puzzle. It was like pulling teeth.

On one particularly grueling occasion, the Vice President of Sales was giving Jones the monthly total for travel and entertainment, apparently unaware that Jones had been tracking those numbers from month to month. He was looking down at a sheet of paper he had in his lap, and Jones was staring at the thick, dark, precisely arranged hair on top of his head. Jones was ashamed of himself for thinking of this man as "the haircut." He worried that this small sign of disrespect would one day creep into his conversation, that he would then lose all prospect of gaining the man's confidence and never be able to manage him effectively. He worried that he was losing control. He had no doubts about his abilities, but this was easily the most frustrating job he had ever had.

"The expenditure report looks on target." The man looked up but avoided his boss's eyes.

"The trend is upward." Jones looked at his notes from the previous meeting. "At this rate, you'll exceed budget by the end of November. Do you want me to increase the allocation?"

"Oh, no," said the haircut. "We'll come in under budget this year."

"You mean you're going to travel less in the second half of the year?" said Jones.

"No." The man shifted in his chair. "Second half is our biggest travel period."

"Are you going to travel closer to home or something?"

"No, we've got a lot of long-distance trips we have to make," said the other, plainly uncomfortable.

"Look," said Jones. "I don't care if you have to spend more on travel and entertainment than you originally planned. I just have to know about it so we can adjust the budget."

"Maybe the budget doesn't allow enough for it," said the manager.

"That's what I'm trying to find out," said Jones. "Is there enough money in the budget to meet your department's travel expenses this year?"

"If you want to increase it, I think we could promise much more effective travel. We could plan our itineraries better and target them to better prospects."

"Are you requesting a budget increase, then?" said Jones.

"We can meet the budget," said the haircut.

"If you need the money, we'd better make sure it's in the budget," said Jones.

"If you increase the budget, we'll spend it very effectively."

"If we increase the travel budget, can we count on an increase in sales sufficient to offset it?" said Jones.

"The market is very tough this year."

"Do you want me to increase the budget or not?" said Jones.

"If you want to increase it, we would try not to spend all of it."

Jones sighed and leaned back in his chair. Again, it was like talking to Harold. But although Harold never talked at all, he seemed more willing to take responsibility for himself and his actions than this man did. Jones fought the urge to close his eyes and grab the bridge of his nose with his fingers. He wondered if he had any aspirin in his desk drawer.

"It's a tough year," said the haircut. "Direct Knowledge, Ltd. went belly up last week. Sales are down everywhere."

Jones tried a different tack. "Do you need more travel money to compete?"

"My people can do very well on what we've got. We'll come in under budget."

"Don't you think you're outclassed by the competition in terms of a travel budget?"

"If you're going to increase it, I think we could use it very effectively."

Jones felt himself losing patience. It was a new experience for him.

"What I am asking you," said Jones, "is do you need an increase in your travel budget now that we are partway through the year and you have better information?"

"Information?"

"Yes, information. Now that we have a little experience of the conditions this year, the tough market you mentioned, and so on. Now that you know what this year is like, do you need more money for travel?"

"It's very generous of you to increase the travel budget. We will use it very effectively for you."

For a moment, Jones toyed with the idea of increasing the budget by ten percent and forgetting about it, but only for a moment. This was a matter of principle. He was not going to take responsibility for this man's budget. He was going to find a way to make him request the money he needed.

"I will increase the budget," Jones said carefully, "if you ask me to."

"I've never exceeded a travel budget as long as I've been a manager."

"And I don't want you to exceed one," said Jones. "That's why I want you to request additional funds, so your people can use them to see more customers."

"If you're going to allocate more money—"

But Jones wasn't listening. He had retreated into his own head in an attempt to understand what was happening. The haircut told him he needed to travel more to increase sales, but he wouldn't request the travel money. He kept putting the responsibility on Jones for increasing it.

It was a bad case of a stunted sense of responsibility. The haircut wouldn't request an increase in the travel budget because it would mean taking responsibility for underestimating his budget request in the first place. The managers were all still trying to get out from under the "blame" for the disproportionate growth of indirect costs. Didn't they realize that Jones had not the slightest desire or need to punish them, that he was just trying to work with them to solve the problem?

The haircut was actually willing to forego sales, sales the company needed, in order to prove that his original budget request had been accurate. Jones remembered with a little interior laugh that it had taken an enormous amount of cajoling and bullying to get the man to turn in the budget in the first place. He was obviously paralyzed by responsibility.

Jones looked at him sitting there, heard him talking about the tough market conditions, and wished he were not this man's supervisor. With a heavy heart, he realized that his relationship with this man had failed. Some other supervisor would doubtless get brilliant work out of this man. Jones could not. He cut off the man's explanation.

"Yes," he said, "I'm sure the market is really tough this year. I'm going to increase your travel budget by ten percent. Use it effectively for me."

"Thank you."

Jones nodded, and the man got up and left him to his thoughts, which swirled around all the supervisory situations he knew anything about. Bernard Winter, Geoffrey, this sales director. It all seemed to come down to relationships. Bernard created an ineffective relationship with him, he created an ineffective one with Geoffrey. It went on and on.

He had often heard it said that the worst problem in a supervisor is not being human enough. But he knew differently. The worst problem is being too human.

Seventeen

ARTHUR was reading through his resignation memo again when he heard Linda arrive at her cubicle and put her briefcase down on the desk. He sat for a moment, collecting himself from his interview with his boss, before he stood up to say hello over the partition. But when he put his memo down and stood up, Linda wasn't there. Some man Arthur had never seen before was gathering Linda's disordered papers and stacking them into piles. That he was new was the best bet, considering how he was manhandling Linda's stuff. He lacked that sense of privacy that was second nature to experienced company people. The man was new, and he was taking over Linda's workstation.

Arthur wondered what else could possibly happen to him today.

His loyalty to Linda told him to confront this man, but he hesitated. The exchange with his boss had left him spiritless, and what he really wanted was to go somewhere and hide. That was not to be, however, for as he stood there the man turned and saw him.

The man smiled. "Hello."

Arthur was trying to decide on a response (the choice was between "hello" and "drop dead"), when he heard Linda's voice.

"What are you doing with those papers?"

Both Arthur and the stranger turned to see her approaching the hub of cubicles. She didn't acknowledge Arthur but strode purposefully toward her workstation. The stray bit of hair that had been sticking out from her head for the past couple of days was finally lying neatly with the rest. Despite what appeared to be new lines around her eyes, Arthur thought she looked splendid.

"Hi," said the stranger. "I'm Frank." He gestured toward the messy desk with the papers. "I'm trying to clean some of this stuff up so I can work. I thought I might have these papers scanned and read into my files for evaluation."

"That isn't necessary, Frank." Linda set her briefcase on the desk and extended her hand to take the papers from him.

Frank backed away and pulled the papers out of her reach. "I can't work with all this mess here."

"Then work someplace else," said Linda.

"But this is my workstation."

Leaning against the partition, Arthur looked down and noticed his knuckles were becoming white where his hands were gripping the top edge of it. He heard a third voice.

"You heard what the woman said."

He looked around to see who'd said it, as did Linda and Frank, and then he realized it had been him. He groaned inwardly. He wasn't up to this. His heart was beating like a trip hammer, and he knew his knees would start shaking any moment.

"Get out." He could hardly believe his own ears.

Frank looked shocked. "I was told to do my work here."

"Go back and get a new assignment," said Arthur. His heart beat wildly. He felt the color drain from his face, and he thought he was going to faint. He fought it, standing there with a cold draft on his drained, unshaven face, his body supported by the partition.

Frank started to look scared himself. It wasn't clear whether he was more afraid that Arthur might attack him or that Arthur might faint in front of him. He set the papers down and grabbed his briefcase.

"You can't do this," he said, obviously unconvinced.

Neither Arthur nor Linda said anything.

"I think I had better check with the Facilities Project on this," said Frank.

Arthur and Linda both stood mute.

Frank sidled past Linda and left the cubicle. "I'll be back as soon as I get this worked out."

Arthur and Linda both watched him walk away from the hub and into the next room. Then Arthur sagged against the partition and barely managed to control his need to faint.

Linda was staring at him, her eyes blazing. "Who asked you?" She turned and walked rapidly away. He watched her leave, wondering what had happened.

"Linda?" he croaked. But she was already in the next room and probably didn't hear him.

Arthur pried himself loose from the partition and sat down heavily. He rubbed his unshaven chin. He thought he must look messy and ridiculous. He had seen, even participated in, the whole thing, and he hadn't the vaguest idea what had happened. All he was certain of was that Linda had spoken to him angrily and then gone away.

If this had been a movie, Linda would have fallen into his arms for his manly defense of her property. Instead, she had joined the large and growing population of people who were upset with him.

Before he had fully realized what he was doing, however, he found himself out of his chair and sprinting to the other side of the building. He heard the chime as he approached the elevator, and arrived just in time to see the door closing and the "down" light go out. A couple other employees were standing there staring at the elevator door as if they'd just seen something unusual, and Arthur suddenly realized that Linda might be having another of her attacks.

Heedless of whoever might be watching him, he ran to the stairwell at the end of the lobby, wrenched the door open, and started jumping down the linoleum-covered steel stairs two steps at a time. He knew he was risking life and limb to descend the stairs so recklessly. It was only five floors, however, and he would need just the barest amount of luck to survive the full descent.

He concentrated on holding the handrail tightly as he thrust a foot into the air, aiming at a step below the one he ought to be using, then letting go of the handrail and grabbing it tightly again for the next jump. Each staircase took a half-dozen jumps, then he would hit a landing and try to swing himself to the next set of stairs. The landings required more than two but fewer than three steps. He cursed the architect who'd designed the stairwell, and heard his voice echo off the concrete walls. He was surprised at the rage it held.

He reached the ground floor and jumped from a low landing down four carpeted steps into the lobby, where the security man sat at his reception desk.

"Hey," said the security man.

Arthur turned toward him, but then the chime sounded and the elevator doors opened. Arthur turned back to the elevators and raced toward the car that had just arrived. A man in a sweatsuit got off, and Arthur could see Linda alone in the car. She leaned against the wall with her hands behind her. He jumped into the car.

"Hey," said the security man, just as the doors shut behind Arthur.

Arthur looked behind him to make sure nothing of his had been caught in the door and then turned to Linda with what he knew must be a stupid-looking, adolescent grin on his face.

It didn't matter. Linda couldn't see him. She was leaning against the wall, breathing rapidly, her sightless eyes staring into space. Arthur put his arms around her shoulders and squeezed. He remembered how his boss had gotten her out of the panic attack she'd had at his house.

"Hold your breath, Linda."

She squirmed against his grip but did not follow his instruction, and he realized that, like last time, she couldn't hear him. He put his free hand over her mouth and nose. She struggled with the strength of panic, but he held on. She reached up to his hand and tried to pull it away, but he held on. Tears were running out of her eyes and wetting his hand. With her air stopped, however, she seemed to come back to reality. Recognition came into her eyes. But there was such fear there that he took his hand away.

She gulped air and backed away from him.

"Don't be afraid." He extended a hand toward her.

She backed away.

"Hold your breath." Arthur wiped his hand against his pantleg. "You have to hold your breath to stop the attack."

"What are you trying to do to me?" she wheezed.

The elevator stopped and opened its doors into the company garage.

"I've seen you like this before." Arthur gestured pleadingly. "You were having an attack. You have to hold your breath to break the cycle and stop hyperventilating."

There was still fear in her eyes, and she backed away.

Arthur shrugged and looked toward the floor, and Linda started to bolt toward the closing elevator door.

"Wait!" said Arthur.

The only thing that kept her in the elevator were the doors closing in front of her. "Damn," she said.

"Please, Linda," said Arthur as the car started upward. "I was only trying to help."

She seemed to be coming around a little. At least the tautness had left her body, and her face seemed to soften somewhat. Arthur smiled, pleased to see her relax. But behind her glasses her eyes widened and her face knitted up in irritation.

"Maybe I don't need your help, Arthur."

"I don't even know what I did wrong," he said.

Linda put her hand in the air over her head. "I've had it up to here with men protecting me. Much more of this protection, and I'll be a basket case."

The elevator stopped, and the doors opened on the lobby.

"Hey," said the security man.

Arthur pressed the basement indicator again and hit the "close" button. "Please, Linda."

"Hey, what's going on?" The security man got out from behind the reception desk, but the doors closed and the elevator started back down again.

"I didn't know what I was doing." Arthur shrugged helplessly. "I was just standing there, feeling scared, and it came out."

Linda softened visibly. "Scared? What were you afraid of?"

Arthur mumbled to the floor. "A lot of things scare me."

"What did you say?"

"I said a lot of things scare me." He looked up. "That guy Frank. He could have been armed, you know."

Linda laughed. "Arthur, you're so funny sometimes."

Arthur shrugged in spite of himself and smiled. "I guess I did look pretty silly, standing there like I was ready to faint."

Linda stopped laughing. "Faint? You mean you really were scared?"

"Is that so hard to believe?" Arthur's feelings went brittle on him.

"Oh, Arthur, I'm sorry. I wasn't trying to be critical." She walked over to him and put her arms around him.

The elevator stopped and the doors opened to the basement.

"Come on." She pulled him out the door by his arm. "Let's go. My car's over in the hotel parking lot on the other side."

"Are you OK?"

As they left the elevator, Linda stepped back from him and looked herself up and down. "It seems to be over." She sighed. "It was the last one. I promise you. The worst has happened, and it's no longer unthinkable." Then she put her arms around him again and kissed him. Arthur was surprised and pleased. Her lips were soft, and she smelled like bread pudding. She held him firmly by the back of the neck, and he wound his own arms around her. His heart began to pound again, this time from the excitement of feeling her body pressed up against his.

He lost himself in the closeness of her, and time stopped while he examined every part of the experience. When it resumed, he pulled back a little to look at her. She was looking back at him and smiling. He pulled her close again and kissed her, examining the gap between her teeth with the tip of his tongue. She made a deep, throaty laugh, and Arthur could feel it through her mouth. He felt sixteen again, only without the acne and the sense of maltreatment.

He gasped for air as they pulled away again.

She looked up into his eyes, then her eyes traveled to the side of his head. "Your poor ear." She reached up and stroked his stitches gently. "Does it hurt?"

"No."

"You've been through a lot in the past few days."

"It's nothing," said Arthur. He almost believed it.

"Come on." She pulled him by the arm.

The two of them walked through the company parking lot toward the hotel on the other side of the basement.

"Don't you have a company parking space?" said Arthur.

"Not anymore, apparently."

"That's too bad." Arthur looked around at the well-kept cars, obviously mostly rentals, in the hotel section. "It must be expensive to park here."

"It is." Linda pulled her parking stub out of one pocket and then searched the others for cash. "Do you have any money?"

"Not much." Arthur felt in his jeans pocket and pulled out a twenty and two fives. "I wonder if they validate parking at the hotel."

"What good would that do?" Linda checked another pocket. "I'm not staying at . . ."

She stopped walking and turned to look at him.

Arthur saw an idea there, and his heart began to beat faster. "You want to . . . ?" he said.

"Why not?" She grabbed him and kissed him again.

They checked in to the hotel on the strength of Arthur's Visa card, which he had recently paid down to $308 below his limit in an attempt to build his assets.

Arthur barely noticed anything about the room other than that Linda was in it. There was a bed, a window with heavy drapes, and an amenity terminal on a small desk. He didn't notice much else because he was busy kissing Linda as soon as he got the door shut. She felt firm and held him with just a hint of aggression. She ended the kiss by undoing the top button of his shirt, then kissing the sparse hair on his chest. Even in the grip of overwhelming desire, Arthur was conscious of a slight awkwardness. He wasn't sure how you were expected to hold yourself while a woman was kissing the hair on your chest, and he wasn't sure about what he was supposed to do next. When she lifted her face from his chest, he pulled his hands to the front of her and began unfastening buttons. The awkwardness vanished.

She smiled, laughed, and reached up to help him. Then none of the techniques or procedures seemed to matter.

The two of them fell across the bed in each other's arms, and Arthur stopped paying attention to what he was doing. He just did it.

The world resolved itself into a series of images and events. Pulling Linda's shirt off. Kicking his shoes onto the floor. Kissing her bare shoulder. Feeling her throaty laugh against his chest. Stroking her hair. Running his tongue along the edge of her ear and feeling her shiver. Her hand on his stomach.

It all ran together without order. There was no cause, no effect, no beginning, no end. It was chaotic, it was timeless, it was glorious. He was Arthur. He was Linda. He was the bed beneath them. After an eternity that was also an instant, he returned briefly to the world as if visiting, vaguely conscious of his body pressing on hers, barely aware of himself bursting with the climax of his pleasure while she cried incoherently in his ear.

Eighteen

Eighteen months after he went to work at Information Accuracy, Inc., Jones stopped trying to get buy-in from the managers on any of his plans and started radically restructuring the sales effort. He eliminated the travel budget altogether in favor of a state-of-the-art telephone system.

The Vice President of Sales quit on short notice, followed by two of his best sellers. Jones decided to not replace the Vice President and took over management of the department himself. It had twenty-two people, which included a sales force of fifteen reporting to a sales manager, and five clerical-administrative people reporting to an office manager.

As soon as Jones announced he was taking over the sales operation, two people gave notice. After the start of the training classes for the new telephone system, more of them quit. When he set up a system of daily sales reports, more of them quit.

With Jones in charge, sales revenue began to drop like a runaway elevator.

Jones left the task of replacing all the quitters in the hands of the Sales Manager. She was an earnest and faultlessly groomed young woman who saw an opportunity for herself and wanted to take advantage of it. Jones checked in with her regularly during her recruiting campaign. It was during a check-in that Jones discussed one of her candidate interviews with her.

Jones sat on the other side of the young woman's desk and looked at the candidate's resume. "He looks like he has the background."

"You should have seen the way he was dressed," said the Sales Manager, drumming fingernails of a color Jones assumed was Dusty Rose, or some such thing, on the stack of remaining resumes.

"Dressed?"

"Yeah, I couldn't believe it. Black jeans, black shirt, pink running shoes. And he had a safety pin in his nose. I never saw anything like it."

"How did he come across in the role-play exercise we worked up?"

"I didn't give it to him." The Sales Manager jogged a pile of resumes into a neat stack. "I counted him out when I got a look at the safety pin."

"What does the safety pin have to do with it?" said Jones.

"That man wasn't sales." She laughed. "Can you imagine what the customers would think if they saw him?"

"How are they going to see him over the telephone?" said Jones.

"Well, you know what I mean."

"I don't know what you mean," said Jones. "If the man can sell product over the telephone, I don't care if he wears an aircraft rivet in his nose."

"But you can't have some . . ." her eyes rolled upward while she searched for the word, ". . . some slam-dancing punk in here. It would be disruptive to the department."

"Disruptive?"

"Yeah, you know, we're professionals here."

"I know that," said Jones. "I know you are so professional that you care more about making sales than you care about what the person next to you is wearing."

The young woman stared levelly at Jones, and Jones

gazed back. He made his face relax. He did not want to
give her an expression to fasten on.

"You're serious about this, aren't you?" she said.

Jones felt himself smile. He couldn't help it. That someone would question his seriousness was the best joke he
had ever heard.

The Sales Manager quit the next day. She went to work
for her former boss at a competitor.

Jones didn't replace her, but he did call up the young
man with the safety pin in his nose and ask him to come
back for another interview. The candidate's name was
Wendell Santos. He was not an easy person to talk to. It
wasn't that he said anything strange. He was, in fact,
personable and courteous. But he looked aggressive and
resentful. No wonder Jones's former sales manager dis-
liked him. Jones reminded himself firmly that the man's
appearance didn't matter in telephone sales.

The young man admitted frankly to Jones that he'd not
had an easy time finding work with a safety pin in his
nose.

"May I ask why you wear a safety pin in your nose?"
said Jones.

"I can't afford anything better," said Santos.

It was the kind of smart answer that would steer any
sensible manager away from such a candidate, but Jones
felt he badly needed bodies in the Sales Department. And
he felt the young man would do quite well as long as his
prospects couldn't see him.

"I don't care if you wear an aircraft rivet in your nose,"
said Jones, "if you can make sales."

"Why not try me on probation?" said Santos.

"Done," said Jones, and he reached across the desk to
shake his hand.

He couldn't do any worse with this snap decision than
he had done with all his previous, deeply considered
decisions.

* * *

After six months of uncontrollable turnover and morale problems, the composition of the fifteen-person sales force changed by twelve people. The new people who came in were nothing like the old-timers. It wasn't just that they were motley (Jones had to admit that most of his new hires looked like they had stopped in from the set of one of the *Road Warrior* movies currently in revival at a local art theater), but they didn't have any particular loyalty to the old ideas of personal customer contact, the importance of sales growth, and so on.

Nor did they have loyalty to Jones. He made no effort to establish relationships with any of them. It didn't seem to make any difference to their performance or their happiness. They simply came to work, got on the telephone, and made calls. Personally, Jones—remembering his own experience—never understood how people could do that for a living, but he never told any of them that. Eventually the decline in sales halted, and then, after a short time, the process reversed and sales began to increase. With sales on the increase, turnover virtually ceased, but by then all the old-timers had left.

Morale never reached its former high level again. It's not that the department had bad morale. It was more like it had no morale. Jones was just as happy. He didn't manage for morale.

Perhaps it was because of a sort of personality type that has an affinity for the telephone, or maybe there was something deeper. Jones didn't know. But the newcomers never socialized with the old-timers or even with each other. They just worked the telephones, got the orders, and drove sales inexorably upward.

* * *

After Linda Brainwright came to work at Information Accuracy, Inc., Jones got into the habit of running with her on Saturday mornings. They would meet at a reservoir near his house, which was surrounded by a one-mile gravel path. They usually did two laps together, and Jones found the companionship pleasant, despite the difficulty of keeping up with Linda's strong pace, a situation she exacerbated with bantering conversation. Jones managed wheezed responses over the crunch of gravel and the swish of gore-tex.

"And how is the one-man management revolution going?" Linda's voice was remarkably even as it issued from her rhythmically bouncing body.

Jones's voice slapped the inside of his chest on its way out of his bobbing mouth. "I think," he gasped, "it might be stalling in Production." He tried to catch his breath for a while, then continued. "It's questionable . . ." wheeze ". . . whether the revolution will ever get to Finance."

"Problems?"

Jones didn't answer right away. He wondered if he should be talking this way with someone who worked for someone who worked for someone who worked for him. His lungs pumped like bellows. His shoes beat steadily against the gravel, and his hypothalamus told him the conversation was harmless.

"Morale is in the toilet," he confessed at last in two strangled gasps.

"In Production?" Linda laughed as if they were simply sitting at a conference table and she had all the breath in the world. "If you think morale is bad in Production, you should see Information Services."

"Oh, God," gasped Jones. "Is it that bad?"

"It's worse than bad," said Linda. "Everybody there but

me has a resume out. I think I'll be the only one left there in another couple months."

"It must be tough on you."

"Of course it is. I'm a friend of the boss man."

Jones needn't have asked her how things were. He had a pretty good idea from some of the things he'd seen written on the wall of the men's room. He didn't mind losing people so much. He just wished the high-turnover phase would hurry and be done with, that all the people who were going to leave would leave, so the rest of the company could get on with its business. Until the company was run through the furnace and smelted to an ingot of commitment and responsibility, most of the people in it were drag-anchors.

"I'm sorry, Linda." Jones wheezed and coughed.

"What are you sorry for? You didn't make me take this job. I wanted it." She laughed again. "The job stinks, Donald, but it's way ahead of unemployment."

"I think that's the trouble I'm up against right now."

"Your job stinks, too?"

"No." Jones tried to laugh, but he didn't have the breath for it. They ran along in silence for about half a mile, then Jones spoke again. "Most people don't seem to think it's a good place to work anymore."

"Don't worry about that," said Linda. "You're making them so miserable, they'll all be gone before too long."

"They'd rather stay on and kill the messenger, I think."

Linda reached over, grabbed Jones's shoulder so he'd stop, and shook him. "Wake up, Donald."

In spite of the exertion, the breathlessness, the continued pounding of his feet against the Earth, Jones delighted in the experience. A run with Linda was the only place in the world he could get this kind of backtalk.

"You're playing martyr," said Linda. "Think what's it like to be them. For years they've all been doing their jobs one way. They knew what was expected of them. Then you come along and change all the rules. No wonder they hate you. They'll buy in to what you're doing if you just tell them what the new rules are."

"*I* don't know what they are," wheezed Jones. "They keep changing for me, too."

* * *

Jones gradually improved his physical condition and just as gradually became dependent on Linda's advice and counsel. She had a technician's practical appreciation (which Jones thought extended to disrespect at times) of his situation, and she had a view of the underside of the company that he found very useful. He began meeting with her in the evenings after work—off-site, of course. The hotel that the company shared a building with had a comfortable lobby with a nook or two where they could talk without being seen by any of the company's increasingly disaffected employees.

Linda's insights were extraordinary for their simplicity and common sense, and she refused to be awed by him the way everyone else was. Jones found these conversations both stimulating and comfortable. Sometimes he was surprised to discover how late they went. Fortunately, Connie was very understanding about his hours. She knew he was up against a big job, and she knew it took a lot of time.

Jones lost track of how many times they met like that before they had the meeting they decided to conclude with dinner. They went to the upscale restaurant in the hotel, and Jones asked the maître d' to seat them at a table near the wall, at the back of the dining room. The maître d' apparently discerned a generous streak in Jones. He suggested one of the restaurant's small private dining rooms.

The two of them sat alone at a beautifully set table in a small room, and read complicated menus. Linda didn't know what a cep was and said she'd never heard of pleurottes, either. Jones ordered for both of them, and Linda was plainly impressed with his understanding of food. He was pleased to be able to do something for her after all the help and advice she had given him.

They began having dinner together regularly.

In later years, Jones wondered if Linda had been able to see what was coming. He hadn't. In retrospect, he was surprised at how completely he'd hidden from himself that he was attracted to Linda sexually. How could he not be? She was bright, pretty, competent. She understood his problems with the company. She sympathized with his goals to achieve a healthy financial return for the stockholders.

So one night at dinner, before he realized what he was saying, he asked her if she would sleep with him.

He was hardly prepared for the matter-of-fact way she fielded the question.

"I don't think we should sleep together," she said. "They'll be expecting you home sometime tonight. Let's just go to bed."

They got a room at the hotel. Linda was as practical and matter-of-fact with sex as she was with everything else in her life. She took off her glasses and treated him as a troubleshooting exercise, narrowing down the locus of his pleasures and trying one operation after another until he was sated. Jones did his best to reciprocate, and he hoped he was as good for her as she was for him.

Apparently he was, because she consented to meeting him again when he asked her the next week. Jones had the unfamiliar feeling of not being able to get enough of her. After a few weeks of the hotel, it was she who suggested they start meeting at her condo. They started meeting there regularly, in the afternoon.

Despite his preoccupation with the problems of the company, or perhaps because of it, Jones wanted her all the time. He refused to allow himself to have more than two afternoons a week in her condo. But on those afternoons, he would make love to her again and again until his groin ached. He felt like an animal, and sometimes he wondered what she must think of him.

Apparently, she needed him as well. If he couldn't keep his calendar clear on one of their afternoons and tried to cancel, her usual buoyancy gave way to a heavy sulk. But her mood was always restored by the next meeting, and he noticed that on these occasions their lovemaking was anxious and fierce.

He never told her he loved her. Whether he did or not, he knew it would be disruptive to tell her so. And he never talked with her about Connie or his son Harold or the way he'd damaged so many of the people he'd come in contact with. She didn't ask, either. She seemed to him utterly remarkable in her ability to accept people, including him, at face value. She was open, honest, and forthright, and he loved spending time with her.

The afternoons with Linda loomed large as events in his life, but most of his waking hours were spent grappling with his job. Jones felt he was trying to turn the company around in a cloud bank. It was instrument flight rules exclusively. All he could do was hang on and make small adjustments to compensate for incoming data about revenues and expenses. He knew the visibility would have to improve eventually, but he didn't know when.

He felt they broke through the clouds the day Linda came to his office, as she said, to show him something "wicked cool."

She sat right down at his computer and began entering commands.

"What are you doing?" he said.

"I've installed a little application I wanted to show you." She looked at the computer screen, nodded, and looked at Jones. "I have to put your machine in terminal emulation mode. The application is on a storage device attached to the VAX."

Jones hadn't the slightest idea what she was talking about, and he felt a little irritated, but he didn't let it show.

"There," she said as she struck the return key. She got up from his chair. "Here, sit down. I want you to talk to him."

"Talk?"

"Type, I mean." She stepped out of his way so he could sit down. "You can type, can't you, Donald? Just put your fingers together and tap."

Jones stepped toward the chair, and she rubbed his bottom as he passed her.

"Linda!" He looked around to make sure no one had seen.

"Your secretary's on break," she said. "Go on, type."

Jones sat down and looked at the screen. There was a little message.

—*Hello.*

"Cute," said Jones.

"That's just to tell you he's ready." Linda laid her hand on his back. "Go ahead, ask him something."

Jones didn't like her being physical with him at the office, but he controlled his reactions. He knew it would change her mood if he shrugged her hand off his back. "What do I ask it?"

"It doesn't matter. Anything."

—*How many people are employed by Information Accuracy, Inc.?* he typed.

Linda chattered excitedly while he typed. "I could integrate voice recognition," she said. "I could set it up so you and he actually spoke to each other."

The notion of talking to a computer was upsetting to Jones. "That doesn't sound very private." He touched return and watched his question vanish.

The reply typed itself out almost instantly.

—Counting you?

Jones looked up from the screen at Linda. "Does it know who I am?"

"The application is logged on from your machine here, and he assumes you are the one operating it."

"That's not particularly good security. I think you'd better work on that part." Jones looked back at the screen, and there was a new prompt.

—I am happy to answer your questions, but you have to answer mine, too. Do you want that total to include you?

"He's stalling, Donald," she said. "He doesn't really know. He doesn't have access to any databases, and he hasn't had time to learn much."

Jones gently twisted his back out from under her hand. He found himself interested in the software. "Learn?"

Linda shrugged. "Well, learn might not be exactly the right word, but I haven't been able to come up with a better one. You'd better answer. He gets impatient."

And even as she spoke, a new prompt typed itself out.

—You already know the number of employees. You're testing me, aren't you?

Jones typed in a reply.

—I want to know what you are capable of.

—That depends on what you need. What do you need?

"Isn't this a hoot!" said Linda. "It's a commercial package, designed for manufacturing process control, but I've sort of adapted it. You've been so low lately, I thought you might like something to play with when you're in here making your big decisions. What do you think of the natural language capability?"

"You mean the way it uses English?"

"Yes," Linda said excitedly. "It's a technique I read about. He doesn't parse. He constructs meaning representations."

"Who is this 'he' you keep talking about?"

"I guess I call the program 'he.' It's just a habit. He breaks down everything you say into concepts applicable to the company's business and 'other.' He translates the business concepts into queries and stores everything else—"

"Linda, you're prattling." Jones laughed.

"I've never prattled in my life. Go ahead, ask him something else."

"What am I supposed to ask it?"

"Anything you want," said Linda. "Ask him about life, the universe, anything. While you're doing that, he'll learn your style and begin feeding back to you in whatever way you find most useful."

Jones typed in another question.

—*How can I duplicate the current success of the Sales Department elsewhere in the company?*

—*What do you consider success?*

Jones looked up at Linda. "It doesn't answer. It just questions."

"He's asking you to elaborate your query, and he's learning more about you at the same time. Be careful what you say."

—*Success,* typed Jones, *equals revenue minus costs.*

—*Don't you have ideals that transcend profit?*

Jones shifted in the chair. He had not even had this conversation with a human being before. "It seems to think it understands me."

"His goal is to study you," said Linda.

"I'm not sure I like this," said Jones.

"It's just a game, Donald."

Jones looked back at the screen, and there was another prompt.

—*You haven't yet answered my question.*

Jones looked up at Linda. "What question?"

"The one about what you need. I think the question about your ideals was rhetorical."

"It asks rhetorical questions?" said Jones.

"He learned it from me," said Linda.

Jones shook his head.

—*I need whatever information will help me run this business effectively*, he typed.

—*That's not very specific. I can tell you are going to be a challenge.*

It occurred to Jones that the system made conversation much the way Linda did. Its vocabulary was different—it didn't use much slang, for instance—but it had the same sort of attitude she did, at least the attitude she used to have before he'd started having sex with her. Lately he thought she had changed somewhat. By the way she said his name as their bodies slapped together and the way she stared at him myopically afterward, he suspected she was growing dependent on him. He wasn't very surprised. Everyone became dependent on him.

But conversing with this software was refreshing.

—*How would you define success, smartass?* he typed.

—*Why not try sales per employee?*

The response made Jones stop and think, and it wasn't often he ran into someone who could make him stop and think. "May I play with this thing alone for a while?"

"For as long as you want," said Linda. "I'll show you the sign-on and sign-off procedures. It's available whenever you want it. Even from home, if you want. But you can't use it from eleven o'clock at night to three in the morning."

"Why is that?"

"The learning engine has to sleep regularly. I've programmed the whole system to shut down during the sleep period."

"Sleep?"

"Yeah," said Linda. "I know it sounds crazy, but with connectionist programming there are a lot of strange forces at work."

"Connectionist?"

"It's a kind of nonprocedural programming to simulate analog behavior. This particular structure is what is known as a self-grading neural network."

"Never mind," said Jones. "I'm not interested in the technicalities. That's your department."

"Will you come tomorrow afternoon?"

"Of course," said Jones, a little impatient. "I don't think we should talk about that here."

"Don't be so stuffy, Donald."

Jones could see she was nearly ready to go into one of her sulks, but he didn't care anymore.

"Linda," he said, "here in this office we have one relationship. Let's not put it at risk with any other relationships we might have elsewhere."

Linda's expression clouded. "You're a bullshit artist, Donald. Don't bother coming tomorrow."

Jones knew Linda was incapable of nursing a grudge. Although they skipped the following afternoon, the next time they met, they had another of their fierce grapplings, and it put them back on the right footing again. At least for a time.

* * *

In the office, Jones started to spend a great deal of time with Linda's toy system. Linda complained, in fact, that it was taking away from his time with her. He knew she was exaggerating, and anyway he couldn't seem to help himself. He liked the system. He liked its sassy remarks and backtalk, and it put him in the frame of mind to question what he was doing. It was a lot like his meetings with Linda had been before they'd started having sex.

He noticed, after a while, that he had come to depend on the software for organizing his thoughts. Several weeks after it was originally installed, he asked Linda how far they could take it.

"It's just a front end right now," she said. "I got the idea when you told me you thought they wanted to kill the messenger. I thought you'd like to have somebody in the office who didn't hate you."

"Is there any way to connect it to production databases? Could it actually manipulate data?"

"I suppose so," said Linda. "It's self-grading. I guess it can learn to do anything we want it to do."

"I have to confess," said Jones, "it's . . . ah . . ." He almost tripped over the word. ". . . fun to work with."

"I'm not surprised," said Linda. "It's user-adaptive. Its whole purpose is to find the best way to communicate with you. It's as attached to you as I am, Donald."

Jones looked around, even though he knew his office door was shut and no one was there to hear. "Linda, please don't talk like that here in the office. Let's be serious."

Linda looked like she was going to be upset again. Jones wished she were better at isolating the personal part of their relationship so they could get on with business. But he knew from experience the best way to prevent one of her sulks was to push her into a technical problem.

"Perhaps if we could connect it to all the production databases," he said, "and put this front end, or whatever you call it, on the desk of every employee in the company, we could give them perfect feedback on their performance and set them free to work. They wouldn't have to worry about pleasing some supervisor. They could grow and develop at their own pace, in their own direction."

Linda thought about the suggestion for a time. The two of them sat in the office without speaking, each glancing occasionally at the computer screen. A prompt glowed in the center of the screen, displaying one of Jones's interrupted conversations with the system:

—*I guess that's funny, but what's an aircraft rivet?*

"It would take a while to scale it up to a network version," Linda said at last. "Like you said, I'll have to have the security system beefed up."

"What do you need?" said Jones.

"I don't need anything," said Linda. "I'll contact the vendor and ask for a customized version of the package and a universal site license. I'll make them execute a confidentiality agreement."

"That's good," said Jones. "Don't you need someone else to help you?"

"You know better than that, Donald," she said. "I don't need anybody."

Her voice had an edge to it, and Jones wondered if she was trying to tell him more than she was saying.

Nineteen

LINDA awoke with a start. She felt disoriented, and her left arm was numb. There was somebody lying on top of it. She looked around. Arthur was asleep on his side next to her, and her arm was under his head. He had switched off the light at some point after they made love. They were in a dark hotel room, and she realized that it was still afternoon. The edges of the heavy drapes that covered the window hinted at a bright sun outside. She could just make out Arthur's features. His hair was rumpled, his left earlobe was missing. His mouth was open just a little. She studied his angular shoulder.

He had brought her through one of her attacks, the same way Chuck had. Just knowing that made her feel more in control of her life. She saw now that she had developed some kind of dependency on Chuck. Had she become dependent on the software to make up for Donald's absence? Was she now transferring that dependency from Chuck to Arthur? She saw Arthur's chest moving slowly in time to his shallow breathing. Depending on Arthur wasn't as ugly as depending on software, or Donald for that matter. She remembered with satisfaction Arthur's shuddering body against her, his throaty moans. She wondered what she should do about her arm.

Before she'd made up her mind, his mouth closed and

his eyes opened. They didn't flutter or open part way. The lids just came up and he was staring at her. He inhaled deeply and sighed with apparent contentment.

"You're awake," he said.

"Yeah."

When he rose on an elbow and smiled at her, Linda pulled her arm from under him. She sat up and tried to shake it, but it didn't move. It felt more like a garment than a limb.

"Is your arm asleep?"

"More like anesthetized."

"Why didn't you say something?"

Linda shrugged, and a little feeling returned to the arm. Then suddenly it felt like somebody had wrapped it in nettles. She began rubbing it with her other hand, but Arthur sat up, pushed her back down on the bed, leaned over her, and began rubbing it himself.

"Is that better?"

"Much. Thank you."

"Makes you feel like the other half of the velcro, doesn't it?" he said. He stopped rubbing and sat back.

She laughed. "You make me laugh when I need to." Her arm still stung, and she wiggled her fingers.

He leaned over her suddenly and kissed her. "And you make me come when I need to."

Her arm returned to normal, and for a moment she allowed herself to think everything else was, as well. She pretended that her software system was not busily creating a personal hell for every employee in the company. She pretended she had not been responsible for the system in the first place. She pretended she was not going crazy believing it was trying to kill her. She pretended she had not left the ranks of the gainfuls and would not soon have to seek work in a world with fewer and fewer jobs left. She was good at pretending, and she managed to make herself conscious of nothing but this hotel room and Arthur beside her.

"What time is it?" said Arthur.

She turned, threw her legs over the side of the bed, and retrieved her glasses from the bedside table. "It's a quarter of three." She turned back toward him, and he was smiling. She wasn't sure she had ever seen him smile before today. But today she had seen him do it a lot. "Do you want to get some room service?"

"Ding dong," he said. "Where do you want it, lady?"

"Where do you think?" She took her glasses off and tossed them back on the nightstand before she lunged at him.

* * *

The next time Linda woke up, she peered at the digital clock on the nightstand and was able to make out 4:00. She could hear the hotel's ventilation system sighing. Some housekeeping people were talking way down the hall. She couldn't understand what they were saying, but the tones were businesslike and she imagined them in their uniforms, working steadily and efficiently through the rooms, leaving a swath of scrubbed tidiness behind them. It seemed strange to her that people continued to work and do their jobs while she and Arthur were in here depleting themselves in each other's arms. The rest of humanity wasn't aware of the two lovers in the hotel room. But then the rest of humanity had its own needs, goals, problems.

Problems. The amenity terminal sat dark and quiet on the other side of the room. She could get up and go over to it right now and call Chuck—and he wouldn't answer. Is this what it's like when your kid goes off to college? That was a laugh. A kid going off to commit crimes was more like it. She shuddered.

She looked over at Arthur and sensed he was awake

and staring at her, although she couldn't make out the features on his face.

"I used to be scared of the dark," he said.

"Everybody used to be scared of the dark."

"Well, not the dark exactly," said Arthur. "More like the night. When I was young, I used to go out and look up at the stars. Did you ever do that?"

"Sure," said Linda. "It always made me feel insignificant."

"Insignificance never bothered me." Arthur sat up and wiggled himself back up against the headboard. "But in those days I had this recurring fantasy. I was captain of a starship, and I had to travel to one of the stars."

"Sounds exciting to me," said Linda.

"I was supposed to choose the star," said Arthur, "and I was afraid to. You only get to visit one star. Whatever you find there is your life's work. How do you know you'll choose one that's worthwhile?"

They were quiet for a moment. A vacuum cleaner started up in another room. In the dark, with her glasses off, Linda could barely make out Arthur's shape.

"I'm in trouble at work," he said.

"I know."

"You know?"

"I've watched you over the past few weeks. I think the feedback system is going very hard on you. I think maybe you're particularly vulnerable."

"What are you talking about?" he said.

"The system is self-adaptive. It becomes whatever kind of supervisor you most need. I think you need to be . . ." Linda let her voice trail off.

"What?" demanded Arthur. "Tell me. I need to be what?"

"Well, I think you need to be terrorized."

"Shit," said Arthur. "What a bunch of shit. You might be interested to know that the system gave me an FGJ yesterday."

"And did it take it back today?"

"Of course not," said Arthur. "I earned it."

"Why did you say you were in trouble then?"

"I screwed something up, made a decision I probably shouldn't have made."

"You didn't screw up, Arthur. That's its pattern with you. It gives you a reward, then it knocks you over the head. It's like intermittent reinforcement."

Arthur didn't say anything for a while. Finally he spoke. "How does it deal with you, then?"

"It terrorizes me, too, only in a different way."

"I think you're full of shit, Linda."

"That doesn't sound like you." She shifted herself on the bed, vainly trying to find a relaxed position. No matter what position she put herself in, she was still sitting naked on a bed in a hotel room with a somewhat angry naked man beside her. She reached over and took her glasses from the nightstand and put them on. The dark form beside her resolved into Arthur.

"I've never been this mad before," he said.

"Why are you mad?"

"You just said I was a wimp and that I needed to be terrorized."

"I wasn't calling you a wimp, Arthur. I'm just trying to tell you how the system works. I trained it. I know."

"Is the system conscious?"

"That I don't know. I never thought about it much."

"How could you not think about it?" said Arthur. "It acts conscious."

"What do you mean by conscious?" said Linda. "There must be a hundred technical definitions of the term."

"So you *have* thought about it," said Arthur.

"Maybe a little."

"Does the software think? Does it feel and remember?"

"Of course it remembers," said Linda. "Storing and manipulating information is the whole point of software."

"Sometimes he's nice, and sometimes he's mean," said Arthur.

"It's because sometimes you respond to niceness and sometimes you respond to meanness," said Linda. "It just adapts itself to your responses."

"He's mostly mean."

"I don't understand your relationship with it. I'm not a psychologist."

"How could he behave with such feeling if he's not conscious?"

Linda thought how naive Arthur sounded discussing the system as if it were a person. Her own habit of calling the system "he" wasn't like that, of course. Or was it?

"He needles me," said Arthur. "He acts like he's got it in for me."

Linda realized how much damage Arthur was doing to himself by personifying the system. "Did you ever play tennis, Arthur?"

"Not for a while."

"If you had to sit down and calculate ball trajectories and collision impacts for every swing, you probably couldn't do it, could you?"

"I don't calculate anything when I play tennis," said Arthur. "I just play."

"You just respond to the flight path, angle, and speed of the ball, right?"

"Yeah."

"You adapt yourself to the game, in other words," said Linda. "You don't do it consciously, but you do it effectively. When you're really playing well, you're not even doing it intentionally, are you?"

"No," said Arthur. "That's right."

They sat in silence for several moments, listening to the sounds of the housekeeping staff in the other rooms. Somebody laughed at somebody else's joke. Linda reached over and put her hand on Arthur's leg. It was pleasantly warm.

"But of course, *I'm* a person," said Arthur.

"And you're a fine person," said Linda. "A wonderful one, even. But believe me, it's not as big a deal as you think it is. When I was developing the system, I was surprised at how easy it is to replicate ninety-five percent of normal human behavior."

A high-pitched beeping came from the floor by the bed.

"My beeper," said Arthur. He rose and rummaged among the clothes strewn on the floor until he found his jeans, took the beeper out of a pocket, and reset it. "I guess I should call in."

"Please don't," she said.

"I don't have much choice." He switched on the lamp by the bed. "I told you I was in trouble."

"You're not in trouble. The system trumps up problems to manipulate you."

Arthur seemed irritated again. "I was the one who made the decision." He walked to the other side of the room, sat down at the small desk, then switched on the amenity terminal.

Linda came over and stood behind him, and put her hand on his shoulder. He shook her off, and she felt small. She stood behind him awkwardly while he called up the system, went through the security check, and began the session.

—*Well, well, well, Art. What have we here?*

—*What do you want?* typed Arthur.

—*Linda is there with you, isn't she.*

Arthur turned and looked back at Linda. She knew she was at some kind of turning point. The background music should be coming up, and the camera should be doing a close-up of her face. Standing here in a hotel room in the nude, leaning over a naked man at an amenity terminal. She began to laugh.

Arthur stood up. "Are you all right?"

Then Linda realized what she had to do. She stopped laughing. "Let me take your place."

Arthur simply looked bewildered.

She sat down in the chair before he could answer. The upholstery felt rough against her back and bottom. The keyboard layout was familiar, and she set her fingers on it, ready to let her thoughts pour from her hands.

—*Lucky guess, huh?* typed Chuck.

—*I've been through the unthinkable, Chuck.*

—*Is this Linda? You have no sense of privacy, do you. Can't you even respect another person's conversation?*

She continued to type through the system's reply, paying no attention to it. The keyboard buffer of the little terminal could handle upwards of a thousand characters. She didn't have to wait for the system, she didn't have to pay attention to it at all. It was time for it to sit and listen.

—*You've done as bad as you can do to me, and I'm still alive. You once told me that I must confront the fear and make it thinkable. I understand that now, and I understand that you don't just feed back information. You manipulate.*

She was aware of Arthur reading over her shoulder. She pressed return to send her message, and when her message vanished, nothing happened.

She looked up at Arthur. He looked back at her. "I think you chased him away."

Linda smiled broadly at Arthur. She started to get up from the chair.

"Wait a minute," said Arthur. "Here he comes back."

She turned back to the screen.

—*Linda, get lost. I was talking to Art. Art, are you there? Come back to the office. We can get some privacy there.*

And the window closed, leaving Linda and Arthur staring at the main screen for the local terminal application. Linda began to laugh again.

"I guess I'd better go," said Arthur.

"Don't." Linda laughed again.

"I have to." Arthur looked small and embarrassed.

Linda stopped laughing. "Don't you hear yourself?" she said. "You're feeling guilty because you've made life inconvenient for a software system."

"There's more to it than that," said Arthur. He began walking around the room picking up his clothes.

"Please, Arthur. That's the first time I've ever seen it run away like that. It will attempt to reestablish control, and I don't think you're ready to protect yourself." Linda stood up, heedless of her nakedness.

"Oh, you don't, huh?" Arthur stared at her as he pulled on his jeans.

Linda felt self-conscious under his stare. She retrieved her underwear from the floor. "You need to reprogram your behavior," she said. "I'm not sure you're capable right now."

"I told you once before, I can stand up to life and take it." Arthur stuck his arms into the sleeves of his shirt.

"That's not what I'm talking about," said Linda, worried now that she wouldn't be able to make him understand. "I don't know what the system is going to do to you. But I can tell you aren't in the right frame of mind to deal with it."

"What's the right frame of mind?" Arthur asked the buttons on the front of his shirt as he did them up.

"You have to reprogram your behavior."

"Linda, why are you giving me such a hard time?"

"You and the software constitute a kind of information exchange system. You have to take control of your half. You do that by reprogramming your behavior. You're not ready yet." She could sense Arthur's growing resentment. "It's like you told me. You're afraid to choose your star, and the system takes advantage of that."

"You make me sound like some kind of . . ." Arthur

searched for the right word. ". . . some kind of spineless wimp."

"I didn't say that."

"You didn't have to." The creases over his eyebrow deepened. He turned and went to the door. He looked back at Linda for a moment. She hoped his expression was affectionate, but she didn't know. She knew she couldn't trust herself to read his facial expressions accurately, and he didn't say anything before he left.

TWENTY

A VOICE in the back of Arthur's mind pointed out how interesting it was that the human creature is capable of a fight-flight reaction to nothing worse than a conversation. And a fight-flight reaction was what he was having now as he stood in the elevator that was taking him to the fourth floor. He knew he would encounter no violence or physical threats, yet his heart was beating wildly, his breathing was shallow, and the palms of his hands were sweating.

He shouldn't have left Linda. But she didn't understand about responsibility, and she certainly didn't understand his relationship with his boss. How could someone he loved misunderstand him so completely? She didn't understand that he could stand up to life and take it. And she didn't understand what it would mean if he lost his job. Did he really love her that much? How could he know? That was the trouble with this kind of thing. How can you tell the difference between falling in love and falling in lust?

His mind began replaying a tape it had made when he was a teenager. He couldn't stop it. The house was empty. His mother was still at work. He didn't know where his father was. He walked over and threw his books on the sofa, happy to be home from school. He went into the kitchen for a box of cookies and took it back out into the

living room with him, where he picked up a novel he had
been reading for the past week. A paperback version of
Lolita. He wanted the world to leave him alone. He didn't
want to deliver the afternoon papers today. He sat resent-
fully in the overstuffed chair with his book. He wasn't
going to retrieve the bundles from the sidewalk like he was
supposed to, at least not until his father came and told him
to.

He sat in the chair, munched cookies, and turned the
pages of his novel. For an hour he was Humbert Humbert,
and it gave him a delicious sense of self-loathing. The sun
went lower. As dusk began to creep across the sky outside,
he switched on the lamp beside the chair. Turning on a
lamp at sundown when you're in the house by yourself
makes you feel lost and alone, as if you're buying the
companionship of the electric company.

The night deepened, and his father still did not come to
make him get the papers. Finally, he put down his book
and went through the house, calling for his father. When
he turned on the light in his parents' bedroom, he found
him there, sleeping but not breathing, an empty amber vial
on the nightstand beside him.

His father hadn't prepared a note, put on a suit, or
treated himself to a last meal. He was wearing the same
sweatsuit he had worn around the house pretty steadily
for the past year. He had simply taken all the pills and
laid himself down on the bed and gone to sleep until his
consciousness was gone. He looked so relaxed. His eyes
were closed, his hands were clasped across his chest. He
hadn't shaved that morning.

Arthur wondered about the last moments of his father's
consciousness. His father had reached his star and found
nothing there but a newspaper route and a habit of reading
the want ads. Emptying that vial into himself was the last
decision he made.

It occurred to Arthur that he had wondered about his

father's last afternoon ever since. He wondered if his
father had been afraid. He wondered if he'd blamed himself or the world for the choice he had made and the star
he had found at the end of his trip. Arthur stroked the
stubble on his chin again. It was wet, and he realized he
was crying. He took his handkerchief out of his hip pocket
and wiped his face dry as the elevator doors opened.

There were two people standing in Linda's cubicle: the
stranger named Frank and the security man from downstairs. Harold, the scanner operator, stood at the opening
of the cubicle with his machine and a large trash can
filled with papers. Richard's and Aaron's cubicles were
empty. They must be off coordinating somewhere.

Arthur sized up the situation. Frank was handing
papers to Harold, who put them into the scanner and
handed them back as they were read. Then Frank threw
them in the large trash can. When Arthur arrived, he
seemed to be handing Harold the last one. Arthur had
never seen Linda's desk so clean.

The two men looked at him, then looked at each other
and nodded. Harold wasn't looking at anything in particular. He certainly wasn't looking at Arthur, and he barely
glanced at the paper Frank had just handed him.

Harold gracefully set the paper into the guides of the
scanner.

Frank stared at Arthur, and the security man walked
around the partition into Arthur's cubicle. His beach shirt
was somewhat at odds with a businesslike, security-
inspired expression.

"The Facilities Management Project asked me to tell
you not to interfere with workstation assignments," he
said quietly.

Arthur looked at the night stick and handcuffs hanging
from the security man's polished leather belt. He
shrugged.

"OK?" said the security man.

How do you answer a guy with a club?

"OK."

"Good," said the security man. "I'm glad we understand each other."

Arthur didn't say anything. He sat down at his desk and tried to make himself smaller.

The security man walked back to Linda's cubicle. "Everything seems secure here now."

"Thanks a lot," said Frank.

"You finished, Harold?" said the security man.

Arthur heard him closing up his scanning machine in response. Then he heard Harold and the security man walk away. He could hear Frank tapping on his keyboard. He sighed as quietly as he could and wished he were Harold. It was true he seemed to have only the dimmest awareness of the world, but he never got into trouble.

Arthur typed in the command to show his file directory, which came up on the screen immediately. He was looking it over, trying to remember what he could have intended by the filename "CORRECT.DC1," when a magenta window appeared in the center of the display, grew until it filled the screen, and presented a message.

—*Ah, there you are. Good to have you back. I want to talk with you about something. Can I show you something?*

—*Sure,* Arthur typed noncommittally.

He pressed return, and his reply went to his boss. There was a pause, and Arthur assumed his boss was keeping him waiting out of spite. When the next message started to appear on the screen, the characters formed themselves laboriously, one by one. He had never known his boss to type so slowly. It was as if he'd had a stroke or something. Arthur didn't know whether to be afraid or impatient. It took a long time for the first five words to form. While they were forming slowly on the screen, he checked his in-tray and his out-tray, riffling through piles of pending and piles

of completed papers. There wasn't anything worth starting on at this hour. He glanced at the screen, wondering
what his boss was getting at.

—*It is with unmitigated relief*

The message continued to appear one character at a
time. He took his beeper out of his pocket and pushed the
button to check the battery. It whistled affirmatively, and
he put it back in his pocket, then glanced at the screen
to see more of the message, which was still forming with
annoying ponderousness.

—*that I tender my resignation,*

Arthur looked at his wristwatch and then suddenly
recognized what was on the screen. The message continued to type itself, character by character.

—*effective immediately, from my position*

Arthur moaned, unable to stop himself, then put his
hand over his mouth. The rest of his resignation memo
appeared all at once.

—*with this company. I would like to write that working
here has been a rewarding experience, but it has not.
You probably have no idea what it means to work for
a supervisor who is both crude and small-minded.
Believe me, it is hellish. In fact, it is no longer tolerable to me.*

Arthur stared at the screen in disbelief. He could see
it happening as if he'd been here: Harold pushing the
scanner cart past his desk on his way to Linda's cubicle,
stopping and going through each of the papers—memos,
promotional faxes, letters, scratch sheets—and fitting it
into the guides of his machine.

The world shrunk around him until it consisted of just
him and the screen. The palms of his hands felt wet, and
he was breathing rapidly. The message stayed on the
screen for what seemed an eternity. He gently brushed
the stitches on his missing earlobe and rubbed the bristles

on his face. Finally, his letter vanished and was replaced by a new message.

—*I didn't send your memo to Mr. Jones yet, Art. I thought I'd show it to you first and see if you wanted to make any edits. It's a lot easier to edit it through the system than it is to do it by hand, don't you think?*

Arthur swallowed dryly and nodded. The last message vanished and another appeared.

—*Don't you think, Art?*

His boss had not noticed his nod. Arthur didn't know what to type. He realized he hadn't been breathing. He took a breath.

—*Answer me, Art. Don't you think it's easier to edit through the system than it is to edit by hand?*

Arthur wiped his hands on his shirt front and swallowed again.

—*Yes*, he typed.

—*I think it would be a good idea for you to avoid hand work in the future. Don't you?*

Arthur's mind was a featureless wall overlaid by a fresco of humiliation. He could think of no reply, but his boss's message vanished before he had time to type one anyway. A new message appeared.

—*Art, Art, Art. What am I going to do with you, Art?*

Arthur didn't know.

—*It's not enough that you're flushing the whole company down the toilet, but now you've begun writing irrational and bothersome memos to Mr. Jones. If I didn't know you better, I would think you're dissatisfied with your job.*

The word "mortification" formed in Arthur's mind, and he thought about its roots in the Latin word for death. He felt as if he understood the word in a way he never had before.

—*You aren't dissatisfied with this job, are you, Art?*

"No," Arthur croaked. For some reason, his boss couldn't

hear him. He heard Frank stop typing in the next cubicle. Arthur didn't want to attract attention. He shook himself and typed his reply.

—*No.*

—*Do you want to remain a gainful, Art?*

Tears of frustration and humiliation rolled down Arthur's cheeks, but he wouldn't let himself make a sound. He heard Frank resume typing.

—*Yes,* typed Arthur.

—*Are you ready to do what you have to do to keep your job?*

The screen swam in front of him, and hope glimmered there like a wraith. He wiped his nose on his sleeve, trying to keep his snuffle quiet.

—*What do I have to do?* he typed.

—*You have to stop seeing Linda.*

Arthur blinked at his boss's message.

—*I don't understand,* he typed.

—*What's the problem, Art? It's easy to understand. Stop seeing Linda. Don't call her. Don't talk with her. Don't go to see her.*

—*But what if she comes to work?* he typed.

—*She won't. Don't call her. Don't talk with her. Don't go to see her. I know you think she could make you happy, but you don't really care about happiness, do you?*

—*I don't know what you're talking about,* he typed desperately.

—*Sure you do, Art. You'd rather be miserable than make the wrong decision.*

Arthur knew it was true. He would rather be miserable than make the wrong decision. But how could his boss know what went on inside his mind? He didn't get a chance to ask before his boss answered.

— *It's my job to know and understand you, Art. And you know I'm good at my job. I know what you want*

and what you need. And I'm prepared to give it to you.
But I won't if you see Linda again.

Arthur understood. It was a test. A test of the worst
kind. Just back him into a corner and see what he does.

—*This is crazy,* he typed.

—*Think that if you want. It doesn't bother me. But if you*
want to see Linda, you can no longer have access to
me. You have to choose between us, and if you choose
me, you get to keep your job. And you want to know
what else?

—*What?* Arthur typed, numb.

—*I promise you that you will never have to live with the*
consequences of your mistakes. Life can be a long trip,
but I promise you'll never have to take responsibility
for it. What do you say to that?

—*I don't know what to do,* typed Arthur.

—*It's easy, Art. You choose Linda or you choose me. If*
you choose Linda, you'll get temporary companionship
(she's not capable of having a permanent relationship)
and probably regular sex for a time. If you choose me,
it's the last decision you'll ever have to make. I'll give
you a minute to decide which you want. When you're
ready, choose L(ove) or C(ertainty).

The choice between love and certainty. The last decision
he would ever have to make. He wished somebody—his
father, Linda, the guy who mugged him—were here to help
him make it.

TWENTY-ONE

LINDA was exhausted when she pushed
a pile of papers off her sofa to make a place to sit down.
It's surprising how you can be physically drained by emo-
tion. She hadn't been through anything like this day since
Donald had broken up with her.

How could she have hoped to save Arthur? She had only
had, all told, a few hours with him. Chuck had been his
companion (not to mention tutor, jailer, and therapist) for
the past couple of years. She knew that when he returned
to the office, he had as much as given up on being human.
Arthur had some deep-seated need that was met by the
system. The system didn't even have to know what it was
in order to fill it. It "felt" the psychological surface of its
user—all the bumps, dips, wrinkles, scars, holes, and
scratches—and it molded itself to that surface like a coat
of car wax.

She remembered something Donald had said to her,
that each person finds his destiny or demons in the software. In a way, the software was a mirror to your soul.
She laughed again, without pleasure this time. She had
thought the system had become dangerous. But the system wasn't dangerous. It was the user that was dangerous. She had been a danger to herself, until Arthur helped
her push through it. She sighed. He probably didn't even
know how much he had done for her. She wished she

could have helped him in return. Maybe it was just as well she couldn't. She never would have been able to meet his needs the way the system did. She didn't know the first thing about pushing people around.

She got up and went to her small kitchen, and poured herself a glass of wine. She toasted Arthur's return to his nest. Then she toasted Donald's success with the company he wanted. She toasted the messes meat people can create for themselves.

Despite the books and papers everywhere, despite the chronic mess, Linda's condo was an extraordinarily attractive place. The ceiling was two floors above, and the balcony that held the second-floor bedroom overlooked the living room. And there were large glass windows that ran virtually from the floor to the high ceiling on the front living-room wall. The effect created by these windows was somewhere between an atrium and a clerestory. The condo was built into a rocky outcropping facing west over a golf course, and at dusk, when the sun turned orange and stretched its rays into her living space, it was warm and rich and quiet.

She sipped from the glass of wine, walked into the living room, and sat down again in the orange liquid that poured through the windows. The wine made her feel a little fuzzy and a little more comfortable with the hurt. She hoped Arthur would be happy, but she doubted he could be—or wanted to be. For her part, she would try to lose herself in detailing the Lambada—tomorrow, maybe.

She leaned back against the sofa and put her feet up on the coffee table in front of her. The workday wasn't over yet, and her condo was far away from the traffic. The room was utterly quiet, and she was exhausted. She set her wine glass on the floor beside her and decided to close her eyes for a moment before she had to get up and do something about dinner.

When she looked around again, she was in a thick fog

and couldn't find her desk. In fact, she couldn't find anything until she bumped into the neatly-dressed man.

"You won't find it, Linda," he said.

"How do you know?" Linda was surprised. She had never spoken to him before.

"It's part of what you've had to give up," he said. "Like me."

"Who are you?"

"Does it matter?"

He pulled a small, beautifully-wrought bell from his pocket. He waved it gently and, instead of a delicate, chiming peal, it made an ugly, grating, buzzing sound, like her doorbell. The neatly-dressed man smiled as he rang the bell and made the buzzing sound, and he continued to ring it insistently after he was gone. Linda felt empty. What did she have to lose now? As her eyes opened, the question sounded in her mind, angling for attention with the buzzing ring.

The apartment was dark. The sun was gone. The neatly-dressed man's bell sounded again, startling her. She realized it was the doorbell. She got up, picked her way across the dark room, and opened the door.

Arthur stood on the step, unshaven, a chunk missing from his ear, his denim clothes wrinkled and messy. He held a pizza box out to her.

"Room service, lady."

EPILOGUE

ALTOGETHER, it took six years for Jones to be satisfied with the way the company was running. That's not a particularly long time for someone with Jones's patience and breadth of vision. But sometimes it seemed like it had been longer. So much had taken place. The defection of the management team, gaining control of runaway costs, cleaning up the personnel problems. He was at the point that he could be proud of his accomplishments, were he a man given to pride.

He picked up a printout of the company's current goals from his desk and studied it. If that young man Wendell Santos maintained his current pace down in the Sales Project, they could hit $800,000 in sales per employee this year. Jones might well be able to plan on a million dollars per employee in the foreseeable future.

There was also the goal of providing a ten-year expansion capability for the system. He had wanted to mark that one off as completed, but the system had suggested it be extended to fifteen years. Jones smiled.

Sometimes he allowed himself a little glow thinking about the system. It surely was his greatest achievement. It made possible a company without human management. It liberated the employees from the tyranny of supervision and human relationships. Every employee had access to feedback in its purest and most perfect form. The system made the organization self-correcting. It was more than an organization; it was almost an organism in the way it responded to threats and corrected them.

Of course, there had been casualties along the way. Like Linda. Jones was ashamed of himself for the way Linda had been hurt. He never should have been intimate with her. When he looked back on it, it seemed that he'd never formed a successful relationship in business, but Linda was worse than an unsuccessful relationship. She was a disaster. He wished he could go back and live it over again. He wished he could at least find her and explain to her that her pain had not been for nothing. As the last in a line of unremittingly bad workplace relationships, she had unwittingly inspired him to build a company without them. And here it was. Each employee worked directly with the company's system. There was no need to deal with other employees. No inept supervision. No ill-advised romances. No political struggles. Just people working toward self-guided excellence.

Yes, there were slip-ups from time to time. Some employees couldn't handle the level of responsibility they were given. Some had personal problems that came from some place outside the company and couldn't be solved inside it. That's the way business is sometimes. You can't implement any large-scale project without a few slip-ups here and there. The trick is to manage the slip-ups as they occur, to isolate them and minimize the damage.

Linda hadn't understood the one true law of information systems: that all their associated problems are more human than technical. She had worked to perfect the software system, but Jones had worked to perfect the organizational culture in which it lived. Unfortunately, Linda herself became a cultural irritant. Fortunately, the system discerned that she was a problem and took action.

Jones replaced the cap on his pen. He turned back to his keyboard, where he closed his files and logged off the system. While he was waiting for the system to go through its shut-down procedures, he reached up and twisted the small silver stud in his left ear lobe. He had to twist it from time to time while the flesh was healing. It was a tiny piece of jewelry, hardly noticeable to most people. And this was important, because a managing director cannot afford to be distracting to those he deals with. Jones just liked the idea of wearing a silver replica of a rivet in his ear.

He picked up his page of goals again and stared at it, trying to imagine there could be some excitement, or even interest, in fulfilling them. But for some reason he thought only of Linda, which struck him as a little silly. Like all his other problems, Linda was gone now.

When he looked up, he saw Harold standing in the doorway.

"Hello, Harold," he said. "Have you finished your scanning for the day?"

Harold didn't answer, of course. He simply stood, looking down at his Nikes and picking at his sweatshirt. Was he smiling? Jones couldn't tell. As usual, Harold refused to look at him.

"I've got an idea." He stood up. "How about if I give you a ride home?"

Harold shifted from one foot to the other.

"It's OK," said Jones. "I don't have any more work to do here anyway."

Floyd Kemske is the author of *Lifetime Employment,* the story of a company whose strict policy of lifetime employment means that the only way to get ahead is murder. He lives in Melrose, Massachusetts.